The Three
Gifts of
Christmas

The Three Gifts of Christmas

A Novel

ANITA STANSFIELD

Covenant Communications, Inc.

Cover inset photo, © *Lost Images,* Al Thelin
    Taken at The Armstrong Mansion Bed & Breakfast, Salt Lake City
Cover background photo, ® 1999 PhotoDisc, Inc.

Published by Covenant Communications, Inc.
American Fork, Utah

Printed in the United States of America
First Printing: October 1999

06 05 04 03 02 01 00 99   10 9 8 7 6 5 4 3 2 1

ISBN 1-57734-521-5

This book is dedicated to my readers around the world
who have relished the *First Love Trilogy*, bringing life to
Michael Hamilton and those he loves.
And to the exclusive readers in *my* little world,
who have relished the "gables" books
and kept me believing in them
since they first came to light.
Here in this book,
these worlds are finally bridged together.
This is my Christmas gift to you.
Enjoy the adventure!

And now abideth faith, hope, charity, these three. . . .
1 Corinthians 13:13

One
HOME FOR CHRISTMAS

Provo, Utah

"I know it's a lot to ask." Michael Hamilton's rich Australian brogue came through the phone as clearly as if he were in the next room. "But Grandma's just not doing well. We really don't think she'll make it much longer. Your brothers and sisters are all going to be here, but she keeps asking about you—if you'll be here for Christmas."

"I understand, Dad," Allison said, struggling to keep her emotion in check. "I really do. I *want* to come home for Christmas, but . . ." She hesitated, distracted by a feeling of déjà-vu. This conversation suddenly felt terribly familiar. It only took her a moment to recall a similar scene from her college days, when her parents had desperately wanted her to return to Australia for the holidays.

"Allison?" Michael's voice startled her back to the moment.

"I'm here. I just . . . Well, Ammon has commitments, Dad. He's right in the middle of two or three contracts that can't be delayed. The kids are involved in so many things that . . . I just don't know how we could possibly do it."

There was a long moment of silence before Michael spoke. "I understand, sweetie. You have to do what you feel is best."

Allison appreciated her father's understanding, but she still cried for nearly an hour after their call ended. She managed to get control of herself before her husband came home from work, but Ammon was quick to notice the signs of strain in her face.

"You've been crying," he said, touching her chin. "What's wrong?"

"My dad called," she said. "He says Grandma's not doing well; he doubts she'll make it much longer. She keeps asking about me, wondering if I'm coming home for Christmas. But I told him it's just impossible. The kids are involved in so many things. You can't possibly leave with so much going on at work, and . . ." She started to cry again, already feeling the pain of not being able to see her grandmother one last time.

LeNay Hamilton was not Allison's blood grandmother. In fact, her son, Michael, had married Allison's mother just after Allison had turned ten, following her father's death. But Allison had developed relationships with Michael and his mother that were far closer than she'd shared with most of her blood relatives. She'd lived in Australia for many years, under the same roof with LeNay. And they had shared a special kinship that her brothers and sisters never had with their grandmother. Allison couldn't explain it. She only knew that the thought of losing LeNay without ever seeing her again seemed almost more than she could bear. She'd always had plans of gleaning stories and memories from her grandmother and recording them. And now LeNay's health was failing rapidly, and Allison doubted she'd ever get the chance. She felt angry with herself for procrastinating something so important.

"Allie?" Ammon nudged her from her thoughts. She looked into his empathetic dark eyes. He knew how she felt about her grandmother, and she could feel his understanding and compassion in the firm embrace he gave her. "Listen," he said, taking hold of her shoulders, "I want you to call your father and tell him you'll be there."

"What?" she gasped. "We can't. We've got to—"

"Not *we*," he clarified. "You."

"But Ammon, I . . ." She honestly couldn't put words to all the protests filing through her mind.

"Listen to me," he said. "It's only one Christmas. We have a lifetime. You've got all the shopping and wrapping done. If you go soon, you can come back a couple of days after Christmas, and we'll save most of the celebrating until you return. I have obligations, but I can see that the kids are taken care of and get where they need to be. We have family and friends who would only be too happy to help. I think you should go. If you don't, you'll regret it. And so will I."

Allison was speechless. She couldn't come up with a logical protest. She was still standing there attempting to find something to say when Ammon picked up the phone and dialed direct to Australia. "Hello, Michael," she heard him say. "Allison has something to tell you."

Ammon handed Allison the phone, but she still couldn't find her voice. He took the phone back with a little chuckle. "Michael? Allison's a bit speechless at the moment. But she wants you to know she'll be on the next flight to Australia. We'll let you know when to expect her." Ammon laughed at something Michael said, then gave him the same explanation he'd just given Allison.

When he hung up the phone, Allison flung herself into his arms, crying uncontrollably—but for a different reason. "You're so good to me," she murmured.

"I take it you feel better," he said, and she laughed.

The flight to Australia was long, but Allison passed the time with a good book and some long naps. When she got off the plane in Sydney, her father was waiting, as distinguished and handsome as ever. They laughed as they shared a suffocating embrace. They talked casually of happenings in the family while they retrieved Allison's luggage and went to the private plane that Michael flew himself. The flight to their home, a station in southern Queensland, would take nearly four hours. But the entire thing felt very natural to Allison. She'd made this journey many times through her life.

As Michael urged the plane into the air, she couldn't help thinking of the first time she'd flown with him this way, just prior to her tenth birthday. And soon afterward, he had married Allison's mother, Emily. Michael had given them a good life, which she knew had little to do with the fact that he was one of the wealthiest men in Australia.

Allison dozed through much of the journey, realizing her naps on the long flight over the ocean hadn't been nearly enough to sustain her. She was startled awake when Michael said, "We're here, sweetie. You'd better perk up."

Allison nearly pressed her face to the window, reminding herself of the ten-year-old girl she'd been when she'd first come here. Nothing seemed to have changed— not even the butterflies of anticipation she felt. The station had a way of being somehow timeless. The huge home where they lived had been in the family for generations. She recalled hearing the story of how Michael's great-grandfather, Jess Davies, had built it around 1880, and his descendants had occupied it since. The house was surrounded by so many trees that it was difficult to see much of it from the air. Spreading out from the yard were stables, corrals, the boys' home that was owned by the family, as well as endless acreage that drifted into the nearby mountains of the Great Dividing Range.

In a well-practiced ritual, Michael circled the plane low over the station, as if to let everyone know they had arrived. He landed the plane on a nearby airstrip that he'd told her was cleared in the fifties, when his grandfather had tired of having planes parked in the field close to the house.

With the plane safely in the hangar, they drove the ten minutes to the house.

"I hope you don't get too bored the next few days," Michael said. "Everyone has a lot going on elsewhere. I'm afraid we won't be around much, so you'll mostly be left on your own. By the end of the week, family will start pouring in, and then you'll get no peace at all."

"Oh, I've got plenty to keep me occupied in the meantime," she said. "I'm hoping to spend as much time with Grandma as I possibly can." She didn't add that having some exclusive time with LeNay would be an answer to many prayers.

Michael chuckled. "She is going to be so thrilled to see you." His laugh became deeper. "I didn't tell her you were coming. I thought it would be a nice surprise."

Allison grinned, and her excitement intensified as they passed beneath the familiar iron archway that read *Byrnehouse-Davies*. She knew the archway was at least a hundred years old. The thought gave her added anticipation at having some time with LeNay to glean the stories of when she had come here as a young woman. Allison had heard bits and pieces over the years, but she instinctively knew that she hadn't even uncovered the tip of the iceberg. Again she prayed that they would have enough time together without interruptions to get those stories.

Michael pulled around the house to where the drive ended between the house and the stables, with a beautiful stretch of lawn in between. Allison noticed her mother sitting on the side veranda before she opened the door. Emily ran down the steps, and they embraced with a burst of laughter.

"Oh, it's so good to see you," Emily said with tears in her eyes.

"And you," Allison said, hugging her mother again. They chattered comfortably as they went inside.

With Christmas less than a week away, the house had a feel of the holiday that washed over Allison as she entered. There was garland woven around the stair railings, and a wreath on nearly every door. The aroma in the air made it clear that Millie, their cook of many years, had been busy baking Christmas goodies.

Michael carried Allison's luggage into the house and up to the room that had once been hers, but was now one of many guest rooms. She took just a few minutes to freshen up before she went with Michael and Emily to a room on the main floor that her grandmother was using, since she was now confined to a wheelchair when she got out of bed at all.

Allison held back with her mother as Michael knocked lightly on the door and peered into the room. She heard him speaking to the full-time nurse they had hired to sit with LeNay and see to her needs, rather than keeping her in a hospital or care center, since her health problems were many and she needed continual care. Michael had mentioned on the flight that Betsy had quickly become like part of the family during the time she'd spent in their home.

"You timed it well," Allison heard the nurse say. "She's just eaten and had her medicine, and she'll probably be going to sleep soon."

Michael motioned for Allison and Emily to follow him as Betsy opened the door wide. "This must be Allison," the middle-aged woman said with a tender smile and a whisper, as if she didn't want to spoil the surprise. With all her struggles, LeNay's hearing had not diminished.

Allison nodded, and Betsy motioned her toward the bed.

"Mother," Michael said, sitting on the edge of the bed and taking LeNay's hand, "I have a surprise for you. A Christmas present."

"But it isn't Christmas yet," she said. "I have to stick around at least that long."

"Of course you do," Michael said. "But I think you wouldn't want to wait until Christmas to enjoy this. You'd better put your glasses on."

Michael helped his mother with her glasses, then he held his hand out toward Allison and Emily gave her a nudge, urging her forward. "Look what I found at the airport," he said as Allison took hold of LeNay's hand.

"Allison?" she murmured as huge tears rose into her eyes. "I don't believe it." She laughed with a spryness that contradicted the condition of her health.

"It's me, Grandma," Allison said, unable to hold back her own tears as she carefully hugged her grandmother, surprised at the strength she felt as the embrace was reciprocated.

"Oh, Allison," LeNay said. "I can't believe it."

Allison drew back and looked into her face. "It's true. I'm really here. I couldn't bear the thought of not being with you now."

They talked casually for a few minutes. Michael teased his mother, making her laugh softly. Emily held LeNay's hand in a way that made the closeness of their relationship evident. Allison had to fight to keep from sobbing at the reality that LeNay would not be living much longer. She was actually relieved when Betsy said that LeNay was tired and needed to rest. Allison hurried upstairs to have a good cry, hoping to release her emotion enough to get it out of her system. She found it ironic that some years earlier she had lost another grandmother at Christmastime, and hoped that death for Christmas would not become a pattern. She cried herself to sleep and felt a little better when she woke up after having a good rest. She ate with her parents and listened to their plans for the coming week. Then she called Ammon, stopping to figure out the time difference and making sure that she wouldn't be waking him in the middle of the night. She missed him and the children dreadfully, especially thinking of the Christmas activities that would take place without her. But she was grateful to be where she was, and told him so more than once. She hung up the phone feeling a sweet anticipation of being reunited with them, knowing that she would go home to another holiday celebration.

Late in the evening, she found some time alone with LeNay. They talked of trivial things: what the children were doing, Ammon's business, her flight from the States. Allison was relieved to note that her crying earlier had helped her feel less emotional now. She felt certain that bursts of tears would not be conducive to getting her grandmother to reminisce.

Allison had come prepared with a little tape recorder that she used to record lectures and seminars. She set it out discreetly so that her grandmother wouldn't notice it, then she ventured to ask her first question. "What's the best thing you ever got for Christmas, Grandma?"

"Oh, my goodness," LeNay said with a little laugh. "I'd have to think about that."

"Maybe we can talk about that tomorrow," Allison said, then asked questions about her grandmother's childhood. She learned that LeNay was the youngest of three children by several years, and she had never felt close to her brothers. She and her mother were very close. Her mother was a good woman who took her to church and taught her from the Bible. Her father was a little gruff and gone a great deal, but her mother knew how to handle him and bring out the best in him. When LeNay was sixteen, her mother died unexpectedly. And just a few months later, her father married a woman with two very spoiled young children.

LeNay laughed softly, saying, "I felt like Cinderella. I was a live-in baby-sitter and housekeeper. Father was gone a lot, and this woman had a way of encouraging the worst in him. So the day after I turned eighteen, I left."

"You just left?"

"That's right. I had some money saved. I packed what really mattered to me into two suitcases, and I got on a bus with no desire to ever return. Looking back, I think I was a lot more afraid than I wanted to admit. But I just couldn't stay in that house. Times were hard; there was a war going on. But I kept a prayer in my heart and just . . . left. I was determined to get a job and make it on my own, but . . ."

The conversation was interrupted when Betsy came in to tell them it was time for LeNay to get ready for bed. "If she gets a good night's sleep, I'm sure she'll be up to talking tomorrow. Nothing keeps her perky like talking about times gone by."

"You would know," LeNay said to Betsy, and they exchanged a warm smile. Allison wondered if Betsy had heard some of the things that she was aching to know.

The following morning, Michael and Emily left early to see to some business and Christmas shopping. They would be staying overnight with some friends in the city to make the trip more productive. Right after breakfast, Allison went to LeNay's room, where she found her lying back on her pillows, gazing absently toward the window.

"How are you this morning, Grandma?"

"Oh, I feel pretty good," she said. Then she smiled and reached a feeble hand toward Allison. "I was hoping we could talk some more."

"So was I." Allison discreetly set the tape recorder next to the lamp on the bedside table. She was trying to think of a way to bring up the fact that her grandmother had left home at the age of eighteen, but LeNay started on a different avenue.

"You know," she said, "I couldn't really think of anything I'd ever been given for Christmas that left a lasting impression, but there were some Christmases in my life that are quite memorable. Through the years I've received some gifts that could never be wrapped up in a package, but they've had a great impact on me. And in a

10

roundabout way, I think you could say that some of those gifts came for Christmas."

"Like what?" Allison asked, leaning closer. This was going even better than she'd hoped.

"Well," she began, "I'll never forget that first Christmas after I left home."

Allison smiled. Perhaps she would have her curiosity on that count satisfied after all. "Tell me about it," she urged.

"Well," LeNay continued, "I left home the day after my birthday. That would have been December ninth. I was on the bus a couple of days, with a particular destination in mind. But I began to suffer from a headache and drifted off to sleep. I woke up to realize I'd missed my intended stop, but as we drove through a town I'd never heard of, I decided I liked it, and that was good enough. It just felt right, so I decided this was where I would stay. I had some money, so I decided to get a room and get cleaned up, and then I would find myself a job. I noticed a couple of *Help Wanted* signs from the bus window. But I hadn't gone a hundred steps from the bus when I suddenly felt so ill that I thought I would faint right there in the street."

"What was wrong?" Allison asked with urgency.

"Turned out to be some kind of influenza. But it came on so quickly."

"What did you do?" Allison asked, clearly imagining a young LeNay as she recalled photographs she'd seen many times. Her medium brown hair had been thick and wavy, and she'd often worn it twisted up and pinned at the back of her head.

"I remember finding a little nook between two buildings where I sat down on the ground and lay against one of my suitcases. I was terrified, and wishing I had stayed at home. At least there I would have been safe. And I was certain I would end up dead, or at the very least robbed or hurt. I remember thinking that God had failed me somehow. I had put myself into his hands when I'd left home, and I'd prayed continually that I would be able to make my way in the world and end up someplace where good things could come into my life. And there I was, huddled between these buildings, freezing from a fever, even though it was the middle of summer. But then," LeNay gave that soft little laugh that was so typical of her, "that's when Alexa found me. And it turned out that God was taking care of me after all."

Two
TAKEN IN

LeNay pulled her sweater more tightly around her, wondering how she could be so cold when a high summer sun was beating down on the nearby street. She was vaguely aware of people passing by, regarding her oddly. But there was little to be done about it. Her only hope was in recalling her mother's words: *If you're ever in trouble, child, all you have to do is pray. And God will send some angel to guide you.*

LeNay closed her eyes tightly, partly because of the pain behind them, partly to avoid the reality of where she was and what was happening to her. She prayed with everything inside of her that she could just muster enough strength to find a room somewhere and . . .

"Good heavens," she heard a soft voice, close by.

"What do you suppose is wrong with her?" another voice asked.

"She doesn't look like the type to be . . . well, you know," still another voice said.

LeNay opened her eyes to see the kind face of an older woman hovering above her, just as she felt a gentle touch on her brow. "She's burning up with fever. Emma, bring the car around."

"I'll hurry," said the voice that apparently belonged to Emma.

"Everything's going to be fine," the older woman said gently. LeNay focused enough to see her kind smile. She guessed her to be in her early seventies, with a gentle beauty that seemed only enhanced by the signs of age in her face.

"Are you . . . an angel?" LeNay asked.

The woman laughed softly. "No, love," she said, but LeNay didn't agree. Surely this woman was an answer to her prayers.

"She might as well be," another voice said, and LeNay turned slightly to see a woman who appeared middle-aged, with dark smooth hair.

"Is there someplace we can take you?" the angel asked. "Do you have family we can call, or—"

"No," LeNay managed to say. "I just . . . came into town and . . . I need to get a room and . . ."

"Is there no one you know around here?" the younger woman asked.

"No," LeNay said. "But I have some . . . money. If you could just help me get a room, I can—"

"You need someone to take care of you, young lady," the angel said. "We're taking you home with us."

"Here's Emma," the younger woman said.

"Help me, Lacey," the angel said, and LeNay felt herself being helped to her feet. She took only a few steps, leaning heavily on the arms supporting her, until she was

14

eased into the backseat of a car. "You lie right down there," the angel said. "We'll put your luggage in the trunk."

A few minutes later, LeNay felt the sensation of the car moving. She felt gentle fingers on her brow again and looked up into the face of her angel, who smiled gently. "I don't even . . . know your name," LeNay said.

The voice that belonged to Lacey answered, "She's Alexandra Byrnehouse-Davies. And she's famous for gathering lost souls off the streets."

"Oh, hush," Alexandra said with a little laugh. Then to LeNay, "Call me Alexa. The woman driving is my daughter, Emma. And the one with the sassy mouth is my daughter-in-law, Lacey."

The three of them laughed, then Emma's voice said, "I told you there was a reason we needed to go shopping today."

"It would seem we were needed," Lacey added.

"Indeed we were," Alexa said, and LeNay felt those gentle fingers take her hand. *Like my mother,* LeNay thought.

"It's quite a long drive," Alexa said, "so just relax and enjoy the ride."

LeNay snuggled down into the upholstery, vaguely aware of Emma and Lacey sitting in the front seat, chatting and laughing, as if picking up some stranger with a fever was an everyday occurrence.

"Thank you, God," LeNay murmured quietly as a cloud of serenity settled over her. Then she drifted into oblivion.

LeNay awakened, feeling disoriented, when the car came to a halt. She could hear Alexa giving orders, although she couldn't distinguish her words. She was carefully helped to her feet, but the blood rushed from her

15

head and she nearly passed out. A moment later she was lifted and carried, while a masculine voice exchanged distant conversation with the woman who had saved her. She could tell they went inside, and then up some stairs, but her surroundings were foggy. Finally, feeling a comfortable bed beneath her, LeNay's hope deepened that everything would be all right.

The following days went by in a blur. At moments she was vaguely aware of the peaceful, cozy room where she lay. But she was more absorbed with a consuming ache, the worst of it being in her head. Just opening her eyes more than a slit was too painful to even consider. She vacillated between being hot and cold, with obscure glimpses of the three women who had rescued her.

When the pain finally eased and LeNay found the motivation to open her eyes and take a good look around, it became evident that her surroundings had a feel of opulence. The room wasn't gaudy by any means, but she certainly wasn't in some ordinary farmhouse. She had just finished uttering a prayer of gratitude for having survived this far, when the door opened and a familiar face peered in. She couldn't quite recall if this was Emma or Lacey; they were both near the same age, and her vague recollections were difficult to keep straight.

"Oh, you're awake." She practically beamed, coming toward the bed. "How are you feeling?"

"Much better," LeNay said with a voice that rasped from being long unused.

"Is there anything I can get you right now?"

"No, I'm fine. Thank you," LeNay said.

"I'll be right back," the woman said and slipped out of the room, returning only a minute later with Alexa.

"Oh, look at you," the older woman said, rushing to LeNay's bedside. She sat on the edge of the bed and pressed a hand to LeNay's brow, as if to check for fever. "You're doing much, much better, I'd say. Doctor said you had one of those horrible flu things. But I do believe you're going to be fine."

"Has anyone else been ill?" LeNay asked, fearing she might have brought something awful into their household.

"No, everyone's fine," Alexa said. "Don't you be worrying about that. We've dealt with illness before, and we've been very careful."

"You've been so kind," LeNay said. "I don't know what to say."

"You don't have to say anything," Alexa said, while the woman who was either Emma or Lacey stood looking on, beaming as if she was terribly happy. "You just get yourself better. It will take time for you to be up and around, and you mustn't overdo. Maybe by Christmas you'll be feeling good enough to enjoy the festivities."

"What day is it?" LeNay asked.

"It's the seventeenth," Emma or Lacey provided.

"Good heavens," LeNay murmured. "I don't want to be a burden on you through the holidays, and—"

"Nonsense," Alexa said. "Any Christian in their right mind who has any comprehension of what Christmas means would feel privileged to have such a guest for Christmas. You just plan on it. We'll have such fun."

LeNay squeezed her eyes shut, in awe that she could be so blessed. She briefly imagined what Christmas would be like if she'd stayed at home. Her stepmother's children would have been showered with gifts and spoiled with indulgences. LeNay would have been expected to cook and clean, and her father would have given her a trite token gift out of some twisted sense of obligation. His entire life was wrapped up in his manipulative new wife and her detestable children.

LeNay was startled from her thoughts when Alexa said, "There's something I need to tell you, LeNay. It's LeNay, isn't it? LeNay Parkins? I looked in your wallet."

LeNay nodded. Then she wondered if Alexa had been reading her mind as she said, "I rang up your father." LeNay's first impulse would be to panic, but again Alexa seemed to have a sixth sense as she put a calming hand on LeNay's arm, saying, "There's nothing to be concerned about. I didn't tell him where you are."

"How did you know?" LeNay asked.

"Know what?"

"That I didn't want him to know where I was."

Alexa gave a little laugh. "My dear, it only took about thirty seconds on the phone with that man to make the picture very clear indeed. He told me you were a worthless tramp, and you deserved to be sick in the streets after running out on your family and all he's done for you. He told me how horribly you treated your stepmother and her children, and he didn't feel the least bit sorry for you."

LeNay couldn't hold back the scalding tears that oozed out as she listened to Alexa's animated recounting of the conversation. She had been blessed enough to be taken in by these people, but her father had to taint the experience before she'd even had a chance to prove herself. Recalling that she'd been invited to spend Christmas here, she said, "You *must* be an angel, for letting me stay in spite of all that."

Alexa looked surprised. "My dear, we are only too glad to have you—especially if that's what you've come from. Do you think I'd believe a word from an imbecile like that?

18

I've dealt with plenty of abusive parents in my day. I can smell them out."

The woman standing close by laughed, as if they shared a private joke. Feeling her gratitude increase, LeNay wished she knew what Alexa had meant by *dealing with abusive parents.*

"That's an understatement," the woman said, and LeNay wanted to ask if she was Emma or Lacey.

LeNay contemplated a way to express her gratitude and get some information about these people who had done so much for her. But a young woman peeked her head in the open door, saying, "Mrs. Davies, excuse me, but your solicitor is here."

"Of course," Alexa said, glancing at the clock. She patted LeNay's hand. "You just rest. Emma will get you what you need."

"Thank you," LeNay said, then she smiled at Emma, relieved to know what to call her.

When Alexa was gone, Emma said, "How's your appetite? Are you hungry?"

"Yes, actually, I believe I am."

"That's a good sign. Lunch will be on soon, and I'll bring you up a tray."

Emma sat on the bed to take Alexa's place. "Is she your mother?" LeNay asked.

"She certainly is," Emma said with pride in her voice.

"And Lacey would be . . ."

"My sister-in-law; my brother's wife."

"I think you told me all of that, but I wasn't very coherent."

"Well, now that you're doing better, I'll tell you anything you want to know."

"Anything?" LeNay asked, and Emma smiled prettily.

"Within reason, of course."

"What did your mother mean about . . . dealing with abusive parents?"

"Well, she runs a boys' home, for runaways and delinquents. Actually, she doesn't do much directly with it anymore. But initially, she and my father started the home and ran it for many years before my husband took over most of the supervision. It's kind of a family business. My mother counseled with these boys a great deal, and she often had to stand up to parents who wanted to retrieve their children and put them back into horrible homes. And she just wouldn't stand for it." Emma smiled again. "So you see, love, you fell into the right hands. But then, through the years I've come to believe that God has a way of leading us to the people who need us most."

LeNay inhaled deeply, not quite daring to believe that this place was real. Not to mention these people who had brought her here and taken such good care of her through one of the worst illnesses of her life. Perhaps her mother's death and her father's ill treatment had made her more cynical about the world than she'd been willing to admit. "Well, I've no doubt he led you to me," she said. "And I'm truly grateful to be here. I just don't want to wear out my welcome before I get back on my feet."

"I wouldn't worry about that if I were you. I'd be getting back to normal first. And with Christmas just around the corner, the more the merrier."

"So, I take it your mother lives here with you," LeNay said.

Emma laughed softly. "Actually, we live here with my mother. This is the home where I grew up. I've raised all of my children here, and they're all married except the youngest, and he's pretty much independent. We don't see much of him. My brother and his wife live here also."

"That would be Lacey."

"That's right. Tyson and Lacey's children are grown as well. Tyson oversees the horses; it's kind of a family business, and—"

"I thought the family business was a boys' home."

"Oh, that too. Actually, my father was raising horses and sheep long before he opened the boys' home. We don't have many sheep anymore." She laughed. "Well, Mother often called those boys little lost sheep, but that wouldn't be exactly the same, now would it? Anyway, Tyson oversees the horses. My husband, Michael, he oversees the boys' home. And we all live here together."

"Where exactly is 'here'?"

Emma laughed. "It's out in the middle of nowhere, that's where. When you get up and around, you can get your bearings. The mountains are close by. That helps. I think you'll like it here."

"I'm certain I will." She chuckled. "I already do. You've been so kind that I don't know how to—"

"Oh, hush now. I'll go and see if lunch is ready. You're probably starving."

LeNay ate everything on the tray that was brought to her room, and she downed a snack a few hours later. They sent up extra helpings for dinner and she ate all of that, too. Alexa, Lacey, and Emma took turns seeing if she had what she needed, but they all seemed too busy to sit and visit, which gave LeNay time to rest. She slept well that night and woke up very early, feeling restless. But she only had to walk across the room to realize how weak she was.

21

The view out the window took LeNay's breath away. Beyond the beautifully landscaped yard, there was what she believed to be a horse racing track, corrals, and three huge buildings that appeared to be stables. What Emma had described as a *family business* was obviously very lucrative. There were some other outbuildings as well, and obviously a lot of activity going on. And beyond them were the mountains that Emma had mentioned. Their magnificence took LeNay's breath away. She'd never been so close to the mountains before.

Her next surprise was when she actually stepped into the hall. Until this moment she'd been confined to the bedroom and its adjoining bathroom. But as she walked the hall a short distance and came to the head of a huge staircase, it became evident that these people were not simply well off. This place was incredible.

LeNay sat down to rest from her little walk, actually feeling light-headed. Then she washed up and got dressed in a dark skirt and white blouse. She left her legs bare, since nylons were hard to come by and she only had one good pair. Instead she put on a pair of white ankle socks to keep her feet warm. Then she curled up on the bed again, exhausted. A short while later, Alexa herself came upstairs with a breakfast tray.

"You're dressed," she said. "You must be feeling better."

"I am," she admitted, "although I can't get too far without feeling awfully weak and dizzy."

"That's to be expected," Alexa said, setting the tray on the bed. "You've been terribly ill. Now you mustn't overdo it. Do you like to read? I could bring up some books from the library."

"That would be wonderful," LeNay said, thinking how very little she was able to read while she'd been busy at her continual housework before she'd left home.

LeNay ate her breakfast, then Alexa came back for the tray, sitting down to visit while LeNay absorbed the view out the window. She was grateful for the company and quickly attempted to ease her curiosity. "Where are we . . . exactly?" she asked tentatively.

"This is Byrnehouse-Davies and Hamilton." Alexa's response was nonchalant and matter-of-fact. "We breed and train horses and run a—"

LeNay gasped as the picture suddenly fell into place. "Boys' home," she murmured, leaning uncertainly against the window frame.

"That's right," Alexa said casually.

"I don't believe it. I've read about this place in the papers. And you're . . . Alexandra Byrnehouse-Davies."

"That's right," Alexa said again. "Technically that's my name, but Alexa Davies is what I go by around here. I believe we told you that when we first met, but I don't think you were terribly aware."

LeNay perused the room all over again, taking in the view out the window. Then her eyes absorbed this woman she'd come to feel so close to. The memories of what she'd read merged so easily into what she'd learned recently. Alexa was a well-known philanthropist, widow of one of the wealthiest men in Australia. One aspect of their family business produced some of the finest horses in the country, which was overseen by her son, Tyson Byrnehouse-Davies. And at the other end, they cared for and educated boys taken off the streets, which was under the direction of her

23

son-in-law, Michael Hamilton. LeNay realized now that Emma and Lacey were the wives of these two well-known men. And now, LeNay had been taken off the streets like some stray puppy. She felt suddenly inadequate and backward. The silence grew long while she wondered what she could possibly say to this woman who had done so much for her.

"You seem concerned," Alexa finally said. "We're really just ordinary people. All that nonsense in the papers was a short-lived thing. We happened to produce a horse that won the Cup, the same year that the Home was given an award. It's all really quite irrelevant. We do what we do because it's what we love."

"Well, whatever the circumstances may be, I feel terribly . . . privileged to be here now. I don't know how I could ever repay you or—"

"We don't want anything from you, LeNay. We are truly glad that we were there when you needed someone."

"I'm certain I'll be feeling well enough soon, and then I can . . ."

"What?" Alexa asked when she hesitated.

"I'm not certain. I just . . . want to get a job and . . ."

"Where will you go?"

"I don't know exactly, but I'll find something."

"There are plenty of jobs available right here, LeNay. Of course, it's up to you. But if you have no family ties, or no particular destination in mind, we would love to keep you around."

"You're very kind, but . . . I really don't want to be a burden to you any longer."

"Did I say anything about your being a burden?" Alexa countered. "I'm offering you work. There isn't a person on this station who doesn't pull their own weight. We all work together to keep everything going. But until the holidays are over and you get some strength back, I'm not letting you go anywhere." She smiled as she finished, leaving LeNay certain that her caring was completely genuine.

That evening, LeNay went down to the dining room to eat supper with the family. Alexa insisted, and she walked with a hand on LeNay's arm to help keep her steady. But she had to admit that she felt better this evening than she had this morning.

The house was not gaudy or excessive, but its size and elegance left her a little overwhelmed. A feel of Christmas washed over her as she absorbed the garland woven around the stair railings, and a wreath on nearly every door. The house had a subtle aroma of pine and spices. As they entered the dining room, she was distracted by the beautiful long table, and a sideboard against one wall, also draped with Christmas decor. A deep, masculine voice startled her. "Well, we finally meet the famous Miss Parkins."

She turned to see a middle-aged man with nearly black hair, graying at the temples. He wore a thick mustache, and his thoroughly rugged demeanor was a stark contrast to his manner of dress.

"LeNay," Alexa said, "this is my son-in-law, Michael Hamilton."

"Emma's husband," LeNay said, extending a hand which Michael kissed gallantly, making her smile.

"You could pay me no greater compliment," he said, then Emma appeared at his side.

"You're looking much better," she said. "Come and sit down."

Michael Hamilton helped LeNay with her chair, then he did the same for Emma and sat beside her, between her and LeNay. Lacey entered the room with a man who bore a strong resemblance to Emma. It was easy to see that they were siblings.

"This is my son, Tyson," Alexa said. "Tyson, this is LeNay Parkins. She's going to be staying with us for as long as I can talk her into."

Tyson laughed softly and nodded toward her. "It's a pleasure to meet you, Miss Parkins. I'm glad you're feeling better."

"Thank you," she said, and the meal commenced. Once LeNay became accustomed to having a maid bring the food in and set it out, she relaxed and absorbed the conversation going on around her. She quickly realized these people were full of a sense of humor, tossing witty remarks back and forth continually amidst their discussion of the day's events. Michael updated everyone on the boys' home, referring to some boys by name as if they were his own children. Tyson talked about the breeding and training of certain horses, also using names which were so odd that they could only belong to animals. He also talked about some of the hired hands as if they were practically family. All of the women were obviously highly involved and informed concerning everything that was happening, and LeNay marveled at their knowledge and awareness.

"Do you ride?" Lacey asked, and LeNay realized the question was addressed to her.

"No," she said abruptly. "I've never had the opportunity to even . . . be around horses."

"Well, we might have to remedy that," Alexa said, while LeNay prayed inwardly she'd never have to get too close to a horse.

The conversation turned to family, and LeNay attempted to keep track as they discussed their grown children and what was happening in their lives. She quickly gathered that both families had some girls who were married and having children. But most of the talk centered around Richard and Jesse. Supper ended, and the couples left before LeNay had a chance to figure out how those names fit into the family.

As Alexa walked LeNay out to the veranda, where they sat to enjoy the warm summer evening, LeNay said, "So tell me about Richard and Jesse."

Alexa's eyes lit up, as if they'd just embarked on her favorite topic of conversation. "Now Richard," she began, "he belongs to Tyson and Lacey. He's our oldest grandson—mine and Jess's, that is. Jess passed away just a few years ago. Anyway, we just had the two children, Emma and Tyson. Tyson and Lacey had four children; Richard came first, and then the three girls years later. Emma and Michael have six children: five girls, and then Jesse."

LeNay nodded. As Alexa rambled on, she hoped she could keep this straight enough to not embarrass herself in the future.

"Jesse Michael Hamilton," she said as if it were music. "The Jesse is after my Jess. Of course, he was actually Jesse, too. But he always went simply by Jess. So that keeps them separate, which was important when Jess was alive. And Emma wanted to name him after his father. That's where the Michael comes in. She wanted to call him Michael, but it quickly became too confusing. Michael and Michael in the same house. So we took to calling him Jesse, which kept him separate from Jess. Still, I believe in all legalities; he goes by Michael Hamilton the second. Am I confusing you, love?"

LeNay shook her head, realizing that she had actually followed the oratory. To assure herself, she said, "So Richard and Jesse are cousins, and they're your only grandsons."

"That's right. Richard's the oldest of them all, and Jesse's the youngest. With all those girls in between, Jesse took to following Richard around almost as soon as he could walk. Richard was so much older than Jesse, but he never minded him tagging along."

"So, where are they now?"

"Well, all of the girls are married, having children, doing well. We don't worry about them. They're all coming home for Christmas. The boys, on the other hand . . . they give us plenty to worry about."

"Why is that?"

"Well, Richard was fine until his wife died. After we lost her, he went off and joined the Air Force . . . which was fine until the war. He's an officer, which he assures us keeps him at less of a risk. But I've heard horror stories about those fighter pilots. I try not to think about it. Still, I think it's just something he had to do. He's had flying in his blood since the first time he realized that it was actually possible for man to fly. Anyway, we haven't seen him for a while, although he's good to write. But . . . he's got leave for Christmas. This is the first time in years that we'll have everyone together; everyone except my Jess, of course. But I believe he's with us in spirit."

"And what about Jesse?" LeNay asked, if only to be polite.

"Well, Jesse just kind of comes and goes. He's been going to school at some odd place; I can't recall it exactly. In between, he keeps up on the business. He follows Tyson around on the tracks, and his father at the boys' home. With Richard off flying, Jesse will likely take it all over eventually—just in management, of course. It's too much to handle for one man. He's a good boy, I believe. He's just so . . . quiet and . . . unsocial, perhaps. Although everyone just adores him, me included of course. He was Jess's pride and joy. After all those girls, Jesse was just such a sweet surprise."

Alexa sighed, then she went on to tell about *all those girls;* who they had married, their husbands' occupations, and the names and ages of all of her great-grandchildren. When all was said and done, the only names LeNay could remember were Jesse and Richard. She couldn't help looking forward to meeting these people. If nothing else, Christmas would not be dull.

Oh - Heavenly Dog

Chevy Chase -

1980

Three

THE SNOB

At the next meal LeNay shared with the family, she heard all about how Richard had gotten into flying as a young man. And now the planes were used commonly since they lived so far away from much of anything. She learned that a couple of the hired hands had learned to fly, but Michael and Tyson hadn't wanted anything to do with it.

Talk turned to something that LeNay had commonly heard discussed at home, although the tone of the conversation was completely different. LeNay's father had often bellowed and harped about the rationing that had become necessary because of the war. He'd spoken of that a great deal more than his sons, who had been drafted into the army. But here, as they discussed the rationing of food, clothing, and fuel, there was a calm kind of concern. It became evident that the family had been storing and rotating supplies of food and fuel long before the war had ever begun. If they were careful, they hardly noticed the shortages.

"And of course," Alexa said, "we grow a great deal of what we eat right here. Rudy keeps a fine garden for us, and Mrs. Higson is a genius at preserving the fruits and vegetables. We have our own cattle, and a few sheep. And of course the chickens."

"And turkeys," Michael said with an exaggerated disdain. LeNay was beginning to realize that such histrionics were common for Michael. "I hate those blasted turkeys."

"You don't complain about eating them for Christmas dinner," Emma pointed out.

"It would be fine if I didn't have to smell them all year long," Michael said. "And they. . . gobble."

Tyson said mostly to LeNay, "This is Michael's monthly speech on turkeys. He'll get over it."

LeNay smiled, then caught Michael's eye and saw him wink. The more time she spent with these people, the more she liked them.

At the next meal, Richard came up again. They wondered if he was safe, and couldn't wait to see him. And Alexa was concerned over his unhappiness in being without his wife all these years. Then the conversation turned to Jesse. Through the next few days, as LeNay slowly regained her strength and became more acquainted with her surroundings, she realized that nearly *every* meal was garnished with talk of Jesse. LeNay had heard so much about him that she felt certain she could have written his biography—except that she wouldn't want to.

Jesse was called *a loner* by his father, a *sweet thing* by his mother, and *such a good boy* by his grandmother. Tyson called him a *scoundrel like the rest of them*. And Lacey just said he was *adorable*. He was a wealthy bachelor, and the family had heard about many women pursuing Jesse, but he never seemed to show much interest.

One afternoon LeNay was in the kitchen, helping peel some vegetables while she sat at the table in order to feel useful without exerting too much energy. She'd quickly grown to like Mrs. Higson, who was the cook, and her daughter, Jill, who was currently washing dishes. The dishes were being dried by Rita, who was the daughter of a stable hand. The girls were just a little younger than LeNay, and she was amused by their antics . . . until she overheard them talking about the famous Jesse. They speculated over his habits and preferences, and both seemed certain that eventually he would come to his senses and be wanting to marry one of them.

Between the family and the hired help, LeNay heard so much about Jesse and his fine character and good looks that she practically hated the man—and she hadn't even met him. She reminded herself that she shouldn't pass judgment on anyone without getting to know that person for herself. So she forced her mind away from talk of Jesse Michael Hamilton and concentrated instead on the approaching holiday. She hadn't felt this much anticipation for Christmas since before her mother's death. And even prior to that, she couldn't recall Christmas being so full of activity, and she wondered if her father had somehow stifled the whole thing. But here at the station of Byrnehouse-Davies and Hamilton, life seemed to be put on hold for the celebration of Christ's birth.

LeNay still felt weak and lacking in energy, but she managed to get around and take care of herself. She enjoyed going to the library and found the opportunity to read a great deal. But as she felt better, she found things she could do to help and be involved. Sitting at the kitchen table to assist with the frequent and enormous baking projects was a pleasure. Alexa, Emma, and Lacey all bustled around, supervised by Mrs. Higson.

LeNay also helped make bonbons that the children could pop open to find little treats and trinkets inside. And she helped Lacey and Emma with preparations on some Christmas projects for the children. She glued ribbons on pine cones that the children would paint, and she cut out little stars and bells from scraps of fabric that the children would glue on paper to make Christmas cards to exchange.

A few days before Christmas, Michael and Tyson and some of the hands went up into the mountains on horseback and came back with a number of Christmas trees. Two for the house, one for the boys' home, one for the bunkhouse where most of the hired hands lived. And one for a smaller house on the property where the overseer's family lived. LeNay felt especially worn out when they gathered to trim the main tree in the lounge room. The other tree would go in a parlor where some of the servants gathered for Christmas celebrations. But LeNay made herself comfortable on the sofa and enjoyed watching the antics going on as they decorated the fragrant pine. By the time it was finished, it seemed to be covered with something magical and sparkling that gave it an almost unearthly glow. LeNay had never seen such a beautiful Christmas tree in all her life.

As Christmas drew closer and everything seemed to get steadily more busy, LeNay marveled at how this wealthy family did not sit around while servants waited on them. They all worked hard, side by side with the minimal hired help. She saw Alexa dusting and polishing things about the house, cooking and baking in the kitchen, and even washing and drying dishes. Emma and Lacey followed her example, staying so busy they hardly sat down.

The day before Christmas Eve, the girls began arriving with their families. Alexa introduced LeNay to everyone with great enthusiasm, but LeNay had trouble remembering names. She thoroughly enjoyed observing the way these people settled into the home and the routine, making it evident that the girls had grown up here, and their husbands and children had spent a great deal of time here. The house that had seemed so big and quiet suddenly seemed close and very noisy.

That evening, everyone gathered in the lounge room around the tree, making the room feel very tiny. The phonograph was playing Christmas music, and the family was talking about Christmases gone by. LeNay absorbed every minuscule aspect of the experience, thinking that even when she inevitably left here and moved on, she would like to take some of these traditions with her.

Everything came to a standstill when a man's voice said, "No wonder you couldn't hear the plane come in. You're all sitting here babbling and—" The man in uniform didn't finish before many of the occupants of the room rose in unison, overwhelming him with hugs and laughter. It was easy for LeNay to surmise that this was Richard. The reunions were touching to observe, especially when he clutched his mother close to him and they both got a little teary.

Richard came in and sat down, while the children held back, seeming a little in awe of him. LeNay guessed that many of them wouldn't even remember him, and some had obviously been born since he'd last been with the family. He was bombarded with questions, and he kept laughing spontaneously as he answered them. LeNay observed him discreetly, seeing a vague resemblance to his parents. But she thought that he looked very much like the photographs she had seen of Alexa's husband, Jess Davies. His hair was styled differently, but his face was very much like his grandfather's. There was no denying how handsome he was, and the uniform certainly enhanced his build. But LeNay personally didn't find him attractive. Even if he hadn't been several years older than her, she knew she would simply never be drawn to a man like that. Consciously recognizing her thoughts, she scolded herself for even bothering to analyze such a thing.

LeNay was startled when Richard stopped mid-sentence and said, "And who is this lovely young lady? Unless I've missed something, I don't think she's related to me."

LeNay smiled, warding off embarrassment as all eyes turned toward her. Alexa handled the introductions gracefully, briefly explaining the situation, then Richard said with an adorable smile, "It's a pleasure, Miss Parkins. I do hope you're enjoying your stay."

"Oh, very much, thank you."

She was relieved when he went back to telling his stories of flying over Europe, taking the attention away from her. Before the family disbanded to put the children to bed, they speculated about when Jesse might show up, since he was the only one missing. "I do hope he gets here in time for our little excursion," Alexa said.

"You know he will," Emma said. "He's never missed it before."

LeNay watched them herd the little ones up the stairs, wondering what *our little excursion* might be. She went to bed full of happiness and anticipation, thanking God for giving her such a wonderful experience. Sharing Christmas with such a family was something she would never forget.

She felt changes inside of her already from spending these days here, and yet she couldn't quite pinpoint what they were. She finally drifted to sleep, certain she'd make sense of it eventually.

LeNay woke the next morning, horrified to realize she'd overslept significantly. She dressed and hurried down to the dining room, hoping something might be left out. She was starving and had no desire to interfere with Mrs. Higson's cooking in order to find herself something to eat. She was a little surprised to find no one there but Richard, who was reading a newspaper and sipping a cup of coffee. She nearly backed out of the room when he looked up and said, "Oh, come in. I was just feeling abandoned." He set the paper aside. "I fear I overslept myself. The journey home was long."

"I imagine it was."

"Help yourself," he said motioning toward the sideboard where covered dishes were still sitting. He rose and got himself a plate, graciously helping with hers as she piled food onto it. She noticed then that he looked different without the uniform. Instead he wore riding breeches and high boots, and she couldn't deny that he looked dashing. "Good appetite," he said with a glance at her plate and a little chuckle.

LeNay warded off embarrassment and simply said, "I think I've been making up for all of those days when I didn't eat anything at all."

"That's good then. Grandma tells me you were pretty bad off. I'm glad you're doing better."

"Thank you," she said and sat down to eat.

They talked so comfortably that LeNay concluded it was easy to like Richard Byrnehouse-Davies. He was obviously a decent person. But then, she should have expected as much. It seemed that all of Alexa's descendants were good, decent people who didn't act at all like they belonged to one of the wealthiest families in the country.

Once they had eaten, Richard said he was going to search out the *troops,* as he called them, referring to the family. He invited LeNay along, and they were soon caught up in the projects taking place. Five minutes hardly passed without someone speculating over Jesse's arrival. LeNay managed to keep from shouting that if she heard the name Jesse one more time, she was going to scream.

Following lunch, Emma and Lacey and their daughters took all the grandchildren out to the huge side lawn, where long tables had been set up in preparation for tomorrow's Christmas feast. They set out paints and glue and supervised the children in their little Christmas creations. More than once, LeNay was almost moved to tears at the tenderness of their bright eyes and eager smiles. She'd never imagined Christmas could be so magical.

Richard came out to see how they were doing, and she detected a trace of sadness in him. She wondered about his wife who had passed away. Was he thinking about her? Was he wondering over the children he might have had himself if she had lived? The thought urged LeNay's emotion even closer, and she willed her mind elsewhere.

A few minutes later, she heard the sound of a distant engine. At first she thought it was some kind of vehicle that would drive into the stable yard at any minute. But everyone started looking upward as they all heard the noise, too. Richard grinned and said, "That would be my little cousin."

LeNay's heart quickened as the plane appeared, then circled overhead. She'd never seen one so close before. The children all jumped up and down, screaming with delight, "Uncle Jesse! Uncle Jesse!" But LeNay found it difficult to share the excitement that was obviously being felt by everyone else. She watched as the plane came to a landing some distance away, then it rolled to a smooth stop in the field not far from the house, right next to the plane that Richard had obviously come in.

Once the plane had come to a halt, the children all took off running across the field, the younger ones toddling after their siblings and cousins with squeals of laughter. LeNay could see a dark-haired man emerge from the plane, and again her heart quickened. She told herself she was getting caught up with the excitement of the children, and the obvious pleasure of the adults who were contentedly observing the arrival of *Uncle Jesse*. Logically, LeNay didn't even want to meet this man who was practically a paragon. But she couldn't help smiling to see him take each child, one at a time, and turn them around in a circle, as if it was a practiced ritual. The older children would efficiently wrap their legs around his waist while Jesse held his hands at their backs. The child would hold out his arms, throw his head back, and Jesse turned around and around. She wondered how he kept from getting dizzy by the time they each took a turn. Then he teetered a little and she couldn't hold back a little chuckle, which made her feel embarrassed. But she turned to see that everyone was equally mesmerized by the view.

"Flying lessons," Richard murmured almost to himself.

"I remember when you gave Jesse flying lessons like that," Alexa said, putting her hand over Richard's arm. Richard pressed a kiss to his grandmother's brow, then hugged her tightly.

When the twirling finally stopped, it became evident that Jesse was pulling something out of his pockets for the children. She realized he had come prepared with pockets full of candy.

Satisfied with their allotment, the children finally ran back toward the lawn, and Jesse ambled after them. As this young man in a black flight jacket and breeches tucked into brown leather boots approached, LeNay found her heart beating quickly and she scolded herself. She rationalized that all the talk she'd heard had simply made her curious. As he came closer, she thought that he was technically no more or less handsome than his cousin, Richard, although Jesse was closer to her own age. Then she scolded herself again for her silly efforts to analyze. She couldn't deny that he was attractive, but of course he would be. She'd heard little beyond his virtues since she'd arrived. And *handsome* came up frequently. Her interest made her angry. He was one of the wealthiest bachelors in Australia, for crying out loud. And she was behaving just like the other girls around here, speculating and ogling over him. As he walked past, he met her eyes for only a split second, then quickly darted his gaze away, barely murmuring a terse "Hello." His eyes seemed to say *I don't know who you are or what you're doing here, and I don't want to.*

LeNay managed a nod in return, certain he was little more than an arrogant snob. She observed the reunions with loved ones, noting that he said practically nothing. He greeted his mother much the same way Richard had greeted his last evening. And she couldn't help smiling when he and Richard shared a hearty embrace and deep laughter.

"When did you get bigger than me, little cousin?" Richard asked.

40

"Years ago," Jesse answered. "You've got to stop going away and imagining me as a child."

Richard laughed again. "I don't think I'd be up to giving you flying lessons."

"Not without a plane," Jesse said.

The men moved on toward the house with Emma and Lacey, obviously going to find Michael and Tyson. LeNay stayed with the girls and did her best to help supervise the children with their projects. The next few hours became a delightful fracas. LeNay followed Alexa around, since Alexa seemed concerned if she didn't keep LeNay close to her and involved. There was obviously a great deal of preparation going on that had something to do with *the excursion*. But LeNay didn't bother asking, since everyone seemed so busy. She felt certain that when the time came, she would know what was taking place. When things seemed to be under control, everyone returned to their rooms to get ready. It became evident that this excursion called for dressing up. LeNay changed into a slender navy-blue colored suit with an A-line skirt and a little jacket. She quickly put her bare feet into the only shoes she had beyond a pair of sturdy, practical shoes she wore every day. LeNay smiled to recall how her mother had given her these shoes not long before her death. They were black with chunky high heels, straps that buckled around the ankles, and the toes were cut out. They weren't necessarily comfortable, but they were pretty.

Everyone met on the side veranda, and LeNay smiled to see all of the children in their dress clothes. It was an interesting contrast to see these people she'd come to know well in different attire, but she caught her breath as she turned to see Richard and Jesse, leaning against the veranda rail, talking quietly. They were dressed almost identically in dark breeches, white shirts, and dark braces going over their shoulders. She wondered how many women in Australia were suffering from broken hearts because the only grandsons of this incredible family seemed content to remain single.

Only a few minutes after it was declared that everyone was present, the children began to cheer loudly. LeNay turned to see the reason: a large wagon, draped with red ribbons and pine boughs, pulled by four beautiful horses, was being driven from the stable yard toward the house. The driver she recognized as one of the stable hands, who had sprigs of pine surrounding the crown of his hat. The wagon halted beside the house and the children all piled on. Only then did LeNay notice more than a dozen huge baskets and some boxes sitting out on the lawns. The adults began putting them on the wagon, and LeNay stepped in to help. As the horses pulled forward, most of the adults began walking alongside it. Alexa giggled like a schoolgirl when Richard lifted her up on the back of the wagon and she sat there, her feet dangling. Then Richard set his mother there beside her, and Jesse did the same with his mother. LeNay felt embarrassed when Richard nodded toward her, saying, "You want to get on?"

"No, thank you," she said. "I like walking." She hurried a few steps to catch up with the girls, as opposed to walking with the men, who took up the rear. She wasn't certain where they were going, but she knew it couldn't be too far. She was relieved to note that she wasn't the only one wearing impractical shoes for a long walk.

Something leapt inside of LeNay as they began singing Christmas carols, loud and strong, while the horses plodded along slowly, going around the house, toward the road that led into the station from town. LeNay realized she'd never been out this way since she'd come here. And now she could see that their destination was obviously the boys' home, which was literally attached to this side of the big house she'd been staying in. It had a look that seemed to be a combination of a school and a fine hotel, with gabled windows across the front. As they got closer, she could see the sign above the huge double doors: *Byrnehouse-Davies Home for Boys.* A moment later, the doors opened and more than twenty boys came out onto the huge porch, along with a few adults who were obviously the staff. The boys varied in age from about four, she guessed, to a couple who were older teens. Most of them were jumping up and down and squealing, much as Alexa's great-grandchildren had done when Jesse's plane had come in. The littlest boy ran down the steps, crying with delight, "Mr. Hamilton! Mr. Hamilton!"

Michael laughed and picked the boy up as easily as he would his own grandchild, then he carried him back to the porch. "All right," he said with a voice of authority, reminding LeNay that he was the director of the boys' home. "We can't come in if you're all standing in front of the door. Back inside."

The boys scurried inside, soon followed by the family, carrying the baskets and boxes that obviously contained the makings of a fine celebration. They gathered in a huge room where tables and chairs had been moved back to clear the floor. Under the supervision of a woman who appeared to be the head schoolmistress, they played some games, adults and children together. Then the tables and chairs were put back and the meal was served. As LeNay followed Emma and Lacey to the kitchen to help bring the food out, she found Mrs. Higson, and Jill and Rita. Obviously they had been working with the cook of the boys' home to prepare a fine meal.

LeNay was silently in awe as this family interspersed themselves among these homeless boys to eat, then they all worked together to clear the tables, lining up outside a particular door of the kitchen where each person passed by the sink and washed their own dishes. When that was done, they all went upstairs to a beautiful room with gabled windows, slanted ceilings, and no furnishings beyond some chairs that seemed to have been brought here for the occasion—and a Christmas tree that stood undecorated. The ladies in dresses occupied the chairs. Everyone else sat on the floor. LeNay noticed that all of the staff and the kitchen help were in attendance, as well as the wagon driver. The story of Christmas was read from the Bible, then some of the baskets they had brought were pulled in from the hall. The grandchildren and great-grandchildren of Alexa Davies presented each boy with a homemade Christmas card and some of the pine cones that had been decorated earlier to hang on the tree. Each boy also received a sack with fruit, nuts, and candy. By the way their faces lit up, LeNay wondered what kinds of situations these boys had come from. It was evident that some of them had been here a long time; for others, it was obviously their first year away from the deprivations of life. The schoolmistress brought out some boxes, and the boys quickly found the projects they had each made. They gave handmade Christmas cards and a variety of odd trinkets to every member of the family, including the staff and hired help. These were all passed out by name, and it was obvious the boys had taken a great deal of time and preparation for this event, with a list of who would be coming. But LeNay was surprised when a boy about seven with troubled eyes handed her a little gift, saying politely, "For you, Miss Parkins."

"Thank you," she said, once she got past the knot in her throat. Then she took his hand before he could slip away. "What is your name?"

"Daniel," he said.

"What a fine name," she said, forcing back her tender emotions. "It comes from the Bible."

"It does?" he asked, a hint of a sparkle appearing in his eyes.

"Yes. Daniel was a very good man who was thrown into a lions' den by some wicked men. But God protected him from the hungry lions."

"Is that true?" the boy asked skeptically.

"It's in the Bible," LeNay said. "And I know in my heart that the Bible is true. Perhaps one day you could read it for yourself, and then you can decide if you think it's true or not."

They were distracted by fresh commotion as Father Christmas entered the room and the children went wild with excitement, Daniel included. While the jolly impersonator was passing out gifts to all of the boys, LeNay whispered to Alexa, "Who is that, really?"

"It's Father Christmas," Alexa said, then she laughed and whispered, "It's Murphy; he works in the stables, just like his father before him, who was a fine friend of Jess's. He's a character." She sighed contentedly as she observed the picture before them. "We've done this for many years, but it never gets old. Of course, the children in the family know they will get their Christmas in the morning. This visit from Father Christmas is for the boys to receive their gifts. But the children seem to enjoy being a part of it."

LeNay watched the ongoing excitement as a thought occurred to her. No wonder the descendants of this woman were so humble and hardworking. They had grown up with this example of giving and sharing in a way that LeNay had never comprehended. She glanced around the room at the people Alexa Davies loved. Old and young alike were mesmerized by the joy of these boys who were receiving a taste of the bounty and goodness of life, some for the first time. LeNay wiped away a stray tear and glanced toward Michael, wondering how many years he'd been overseeing this wonderful place. He was obviously enjoying himself. As her eyes moved back, she caught a glimpse of Jesse Hamilton, and for a split second she could have sworn he'd been watching her. But his eyes darted quickly away with an expression that made her certain he disdained her presence. Perhaps he felt that their family traditions should not be intruded upon by a stranger. Perhaps he assumed she would go better with the hired help. And perhaps he was right. But she reminded herself that once Christmas was over, she would either join those who worked here or she would move on. She pushed away her contempt for the esteemed Mr. Hamilton and focused on the tender scene taking place as the boys opened their presents. Each gift was unique and apparently well received. It was obvious that someone had taken great effort to hand-pick gifts that would mean something special to each boy and their individual interests. She contemplated briefly the probable circumstances many of these children had come from, and realized that she felt a degree of kinship with them—although her circumstances, in comparison, were likely very good.

While the children all took to playing in absolute chaos, LeNay took notice of the little handmade card and gift that Daniel had given her. She opened it as she had seen the others do, and her eyes filled with mist as she removed from a little box a narrow white ribbon, obviously meant to hang around her neck. On it hung a few oddly shaped beads, made from some kind of dough that had been baked to harden it. Then they had been painted with little haphazard hearts. She hung it around her neck and wiped away her tears before she sought out Daniel and thanked him, telling him how much she loved it. The boy beamed as he returned to his play.

As the children piled back into the wagon to return home in the light of a setting sun, LeNay set an empty basket in with them, then bent down to unbuckle her shoes. As usual, once she'd worn them for a long while, her feet began to hurt. She carried them by the straps in one hand as she walked beside the wagon, joining in the Christmas carols being sung. She heard someone speaking behind her, and glanced over her shoulder to see Jesse lifting one of his little nieces out of the wagon to carry her. LeNay turned her concentration to the road ahead, unnerved to realize that Jesse was walking directly behind her. Then she wondered why she cared. She somehow believed that this spoiled child who got so much attention from his family was little more than a black sheep—a man who had somehow missed out on the concept of the loving, giving attitude that radiated from the rest of the family.

LeNay found the antics of trying to get the children to bed rather humorous. After they had all put out their special Christmas pillow slips, with the hope of having them filled by Father Christmas, they were all far too excited to settle down. LeNay went to her room to wash her feet, feeling so completely surrounded by love and goodness that she could hardly sleep herself.

Four

MISCONCEPTION

~~~

Christmas morning was another delightful frenzy. LeNay observed everything as if from the outside looking in, but at the same time feeling in awe of the love and complete acceptance she was given by the entire family— except Jesse, who wouldn't even make eye contact with her. He was so blatantly impolite that LeNay had trouble believing he had actually grown up in this house, where kindness seeped from every floorboard.

Perhaps it was her very dislike of Jesse that made her prone to observing him discreetly. Yes, he was certainly handsome. But his good looks seemed marred by a nearly constant expression of loftiness, as if he somehow didn't feel like he belonged among such trivialities. LeNay couldn't help noticing the way Jill and Rita vied for his attention whenever the opportunity came to get near him. His absolute indifference toward them was evident, and LeNay wondered if they had any idea what fools they were making of themselves.

At mid-day, a huge feast was set out on many long tables beneath the trees on the lawn. It soon became evident that *everyone* who lived at Byrnehouse-Davies was present, and there was no distinction between their situations in life except for the fact that Alexa was the one who designated someone to offer a blessing on the meal. She called on Richard, and LeNay felt tears gathering behind her closed eyelids as he prayed aloud on behalf of all who were gathered. The prayer was lengthy and eloquent, with expressions of gratitude for all they had been blessed with, for the bounty of their lives, and for the peace and security they lived in, especially in a time of war when many in the world were suffering. He expressed gratitude for being gathered among family and friends, for the love and unity present, and for the meal prepared by so many loving hands. He prayed for a special blessing upon Alexa, who stood as matriarch of this family and a leader to all who knew her and received the benefits of her loving heart. LeNay counted herself among these and felt her own gratitude deepen. Then Richard's voice broke as he prayed that the war might come to an end before more lives were lost, and that the world could be at peace. His intensity made her wonder what kind of horrors he might have witnessed while fighting in Europe.

LeNay felt embarrassed by the tears streaming down her face as the *amen* was spoken. But as she lifted her head, it became evident that nearly every adult was crying, too. Even Jesse Hamilton wiped a quick hand over his cheeks before the food was passed down the long tables. The meal covered the gamut of good food, including five turkeys that had been roasting in pits in the yard since early this morning to keep the house from getting unbearably hot. LeNay sat with Murphy and his wife at one side of her, an amusing character to say the least. She imagined him dressed as Father Christmas last night and smiled to herself. On her other side sat a boy from the home, who appeared to be about twelve. She attempted casual conversation with him, but he didn't talk much.

When the meal was finished, plum pudding was dished up and passed down the tables while everyone speculated and laughed over who might receive the serving with the lucky coin inside. LeNay was familiar with this tradition, but she'd never found it so amusing. Alexa announced that there were *six* lucky coins in the pudding, since there were so many people present. LeNay picked slowly at her pudding, feeling unbearably full from all the dinner she'd eaten. She watched with anticipation to see who might find the coins. Four were found quickly, evoking laughter and excitement. The fifth appeared after another five minutes of chattering and banter. While LeNay's mind was wandering to what her family might be doing, she bit into something hard and realized she had the sixth coin in her pudding. "Oh, good heavens," she murmured and Murphy shouted, "Miss Parkins has it! Blimey, isn't she a lucky one!"

"Indeed," LeNay said, thinking her luck had nothing to do with the coin in her pudding. But she felt it would be more accurate to say that she was extremely blessed just for being here. If anything, being the recipient of the coin was only cause for feeling embarrassed as she became the center of attention.

Along with the five other winners, none of whom were in the family, she was escorted to the head of the table where Alexa had six wrapped gifts. She whispered discreetly, "Take the one with the red bow."

LeNay followed the suggestion and returned to her seat to open the package, since the other winners were doing the same. She gasped to find a bottle of expensive hand lotion with the fragrance of gardenias. Murphy said, "Oooh, it's too bad I didn't win."

"Yeah," one of the other hands said. "You could stand to smell a little more flowery."

"Do you want to try some?" she said to Murphy, provoking a hearty laugh from those around her.

"Ooh, I do," Murphy's wife, Lorinda, said. LeNay passed the bottle to her and watched as she smoothed the creamy concoction over her hands, inhaling it with obvious pleasure. "Thank you," she said. "I love gardenias."

LeNay pitched in with the others to see that the meal was cleaned up, and all the dishes were washed and put away. The afternoon then became quiet with children napping and the work behind them. Later in the afternoon the family gathered for Christmas tea, bringing out cold turkey, salads, and a number of goodies that had been prepared ahead. The evening was filled with the sharing of stories and a quiet gift exchange among the family that had nothing to do with the earlier offerings of Father Christmas. Each person had drawn the name of a family member to give a gift to, so each person received one gift. Everyone was given their gift before the opening started, beginning with the youngest and moving up. LeNay was surprised when Emma handed her a gift. She felt briefly alarmed, since she'd not been forewarned and had no gift to give. Alexa whispered gently, "It's all right, love. Just relax and enjoy yourself."

Being eighteen, LeNay opened her gift after the young-sters were finished, and just before Jesse. She tried not to feel conspicuous as she opened the gift to reveal a beautiful leather-bound book with blank pages, and a fine pen.

"Journal keeping is kind of a tradition with us," Alexa said. "We hoped you would like it."

"Thank you," LeNay said, pressing her hand lovingly over the quality binding. "It's beautiful. I don't know if I've ever had anything so lovely."

Alexa beamed, as did Emma and Lacey. LeNay figured the gift had been a joint effort.

When the celebrating was finally over, LeNay crawled into bed, completely exhausted and thoroughly content. She didn't have to wonder if she'd ever experienced anything so completely incredible in her life. As long as she lived, the previous two days would always remain some of her most precious memories. When she found it difficult to sleep, she turned on the lamp and began to write in her new journal. It was something she'd never done before, but she enjoyed the experience of recording the events of Christmas in detail, and then how she had come here to begin with. She finally slept with tender memories and feelings close to her heart.

The family members who had traveled all stayed through the following day, and LeNay enjoyed observing them interact, now that she'd gotten to know them better. Even though a part of her felt annoyed at even feeling any interest, she couldn't help observing Jesse. Perhaps all she'd heard about him made her curious, she reasoned, not for the first time. She noticed that Jesse seemed most comfortable with the children. He played and teased, but he hardly talked—not even to his sisters and parents. Yet they all seemed to be able to read his mind and guess what he was thinking. Or at the very least, they all seemed skilled at coaxing his thoughts into the open. LeNay found the whole thing rather annoying. It was obvious to her that because he was Michael and Emma's only boy, he'd been spoiled and given far too much attention. She was surprised to see that even Alexa hovered over him and coddled him, which seemed to go against her character. She certainly cared about all of her family, but it wasn't like her to be so doting. Jesse, in turn, completely ignored the servants—and LeNay, even though she had been introduced as a guest of the family, and she'd been included in all of the family activities and meals.

Two days after Christmas, the girls and their families all slowly filtered away through the day. By evening the house was eerily quiet. Richard and Jesse were the only remaining visitors. She noticed them going riding together in the late afternoon, returning just before supper. They came in the dining room dressed much the same way, in high riding boots, jodhpurs, and button-up shirts, topped by braces. Knowing that Jesse had followed Richard around through his growing years, she wondered if he purposely emulated his cousin, even in his manner of dress. But then she realized that Tyson and Michael dressed similarly. Perhaps, she concluded, the family had a certain style that suited their manner of living.

After supper, Alexa disappeared with Jesse. LeNay helped in the kitchen, then wandered out to the veranda to sit and watch the sun go down, which had become a pleasant pastime on many evenings. She was surprised to find Richard there, and thought it might be best to leave him be, since he'd been there first. She turned to leave, thinking he hadn't noticed her, when he said, "You don't have to leave. I get the feeling you're trying to avoid me."

"No, not at all," she said. "I just didn't want to disturb you if—"

"You're not disturbing me," he insisted, motioning with his hand for her to come closer. He was leaning back against the veranda rail, turned toward the house, with one booted foot tucked against the post behind him. "Sit down. It's a nice place to be this time of day."

"Yes, it is," she said. Then she realized he was smoking as he put a cigarette to his lips and blew out a slow stream of smoke.

LeNay's father had been a smoker, but she'd never been able to see the appeal. Still she was surprised when Richard said, "Disgusting habit, I know." He took one more long draw, then stamped out the cigarette in an ashtray that he'd obviously brought with him. LeNay had never seen one in the house. "I fear most of the Air Force is smoking. It's one of many things they have done to taint my life." He said it lightly, but LeNay sensed something deeper in his words. He added a little more severely, "If Lottie were alive, I know she wouldn't put up with it."

LeNay was amazed to realize Richard was talking to *her* about his deceased wife. She gently said, "You must miss her very much."

He glanced away and gave a brief laugh with no hint of amusement. "More than you can possibly imagine. Sometimes the only thing that keeps me going is the idea of Lottie waiting for me in some other dimension of life."

"I'm certain she is," LeNay said.

"I'd like to think so. I suppose I won't know for certain until I finally get shot down and—"

"Your grandmother wouldn't let you talk like that," LeNay interrupted.

Richard laughed. "How well you have come to know her, in so short a time." He turned more toward LeNay and folded his arms over his chest. "And will you be her advocate in her absence?"

LeNay glanced down. "No, I just . . ." She hesitated.

"That's too bad," he said. "I was hoping you would be. It would be nice to have such a lovely young woman telling me to look after myself and be careful."

LeNay glanced down, then looked into Richard's eyes. She wondered briefly if his openness was an indication of any degree of romantic interest. But she was relieved to sense nothing beyond comfortable conversation. She said gently, "Look after yourself and be careful."

He smiled, then glanced away. "I doubt it would make much difference to you, Miss Parkins, if you never saw me again."

"It would make a difference to these people I have grown to care for—people who love you very much."

He smiled again, as if she'd given the right answer. "Yes, and they've grown to care for you. That's evident. Mother tells me that Grandma has been livelier since you've arrived. You've given her something to do; someone to nurture again."

LeNay glanced away, wondering why she should be so blessed. She readily admitted, "Your grandmother is an angel. She has been a great blessing in my life. If I left here tomorrow, I would never be free of the influence she has given me already."

"You won't leave here, tomorrow, will you?" he asked.

"Not tomorrow," she said, "but I'm not certain how long I'll stay."

"Of course you have to do what you feel is best," he said. "But consider this. The world beyond this place is not so great. There is a sense of security here that can only be created by people who work very hard to nurture it. You have been a great blessing to my grandmother. Whatever you might give to Alexandra Davies, she will give back to you tenfold."

LeNay couldn't speak. The tender emotions that had hovered close to the surface all through the holidays were suddenly too strong to hold back if she attempted to use her voice. She felt sure Richard noticed the tears brimming in her eyes, but he turned to look at the view, as if to avoid embarrassing her. "Grandma tells me she feels as if you're one of the family. That would either make you equivalent to my sister or my cousin. Which would it be?"

LeNay only shook her head, still not daring to speak.

"My cousin, I think," he said. "That way we could share a little time together before I leave again, and I might even get a kiss. But since we're as good as cousins, we would both know that there were no romantic implications." He turned to look at her directly again, as if to gauge her reaction. She didn't know why his simple declaration was so touching. She knew exactly where his feelings stood, and she didn't have any trouble agreeing with him completely. Her desire to spend some time with him didn't mean she was attracted to him romantically. She considered that a blessing, knowing that he would be leaving in a few days.

Her tears spilled before she could stop them. He furrowed his brow slightly, then caught one on his finger. "Did I say something to hurt your feelings, LeNay? May I call you LeNay?"

"Yes," she said, now that holding her emotion back was no longer an issue. "You may call me LeNay. No, you didn't hurt my feelings. Quite the opposite. It's just that . . . you've been very sweet. You remind me a great deal of your grandmother, I believe." She smiled and wiped her face dry with her fingers. "Cousins would be fine."

Richard smiled and held out a hand, saying, "Would you care to take a walk with me?"

"I would love to," she said and took his hand.

Before he led her off the veranda, he touched the bead necklace she wore that little Daniel had given her for Christmas. "That's very sweet," he said.

"Yes, it was a very touching gift," she replied with a smile.

"I mean that you wear it," he added with a tender smile.

They walked around the house, talking comfortably about incidental things. Then she asked him if he was dreading his departure.

"More than I'm willing to admit to anyone but you," he said, which made her wonder if her not being a member of the family made it easier for him to talk openly with her. A minute later he said casually, "Did you know that the average life expectancy of a fighter pilot in action is about six weeks?"

LeNay was too horrified to respond, and her uneasiness increased as he continued. "I've already beat the odds more than ten times that. But I have a feeling my luck won't hold out much longer." He laughed softly, but LeNay didn't find it amusing in the least. "You won't tell anyone that I said that, will you?"

"Of course not, but . . ."

"What?" he insisted.

"I don't believe in luck."

"What do you believe in, LeNay?"

"Destiny, perhaps."

"And how would destiny apply in the case of young men being shipped across the sea to be shot down for the sake of freedom?" There was a tinge of bitterness in his voice.

"I'm no philosopher, but . . ."

"I don't need any philosophy but your very own. What do *you* think?"

"If they make it home, then they're meant to make it home."

"Well, maybe I'm not meant to make it home," he said as if he'd had some sort of premonition. The thought sent a chill across LeNay's shoulders. Then he added softly, "I only pray that this will all come to an end before Jesse's number gets called up."

It took LeNay a moment to realize what he meant. Was it only a matter of time before Jesse Hamilton went off to war? The thought put a little different perspective on all the coddling he was getting from his family, although she doubted that was the reason for their excessive attention.

LeNay was relieved when the conversation turned to other things. They ambled slowly back to the veranda. It was completely dark now, but the yard was well lit with electric lights. "It's getting late," he said, "but I've enjoyed our little outing."

"So did I. Thank you."

He said nothing more, but he seemed hesitant to let go of her hand. She couldn't deny her own desire to linger with him, feeling completely comfortable.

"I think I'll sit for a while," she said. "I doubt I could sleep."

Richard smiled, as if she'd read his mind. "I was thinking of doing the same, but . . . if you prefer to be alone . . ."

"Oh, no. Please join me."

Richard sat close beside her, keeping her hand in his as he placed his booted feet up on the veranda rail. She was surprised to hear the conversation turn to the way he'd observed the war affecting people's lives. He talked of the many young men he'd known, each with their own personal tragedies related to love. Some had married just prior to leaving their brides behind to wonder if they'd ever be together again. Some had lost their loved ones to another because of the length of time they were separated and the difficult circumstances of waiting and wondering. Some had become involved with women in the countries where they were stationed temporarily, leaving behind broken hearts and often illegitimate children. He talked of the desperation men and women seemed to feel when confronted with the reality of war.

"It's as if," he said in a dreamy voice, "a man being faced with the possibility of death wants more than anything to just hold a woman close one more time. Some do their best to remain honorable. Some have no honor at all. Either way, war breaks hearts and ruins lives—even when death doesn't happen."

LeNay tried to think of something to say as silence followed his conclusion. She turned to look at him and was startled to see the pain etched into his expression. She could almost literally feel his fear at having to return to the war front, leaving loved ones behind. She wondered if he'd broken any hearts since the loss of his wife, but she felt certain that at least he was one of those bound by honor. He turned to look at her, and she was embarrassed to realize she'd been staring at him. But something in his gaze was so compelling that she couldn't even force herself to turn away.

He smiled slightly and murmured, "Do you think . . . if circumstances were different, that you and I could ever. . ."

LeNay finally found the will to turn away. He didn't have to finish the sentence for her to be certain what he meant. And it only took a moment to search her feelings. "No," she said at the risk of sounding insensitive.

She was relieved to hear him chuckle. "Your honesty is precious, LeNay. Most women would say almost anything to a man going off to fight."

"Would you prefer to go away with false hopes and come home expecting a woman to be waiting, when she wouldn't be?"

"No, personally I prefer honesty."

"Well then, you should know that I am thoroughly enjoying myself, but . . . it could never be more than this."

"I know," he said, gently squeezing her hand.

LeNay turned to look at him again, saying, "I dare say we could be very good friends, you and I."

Richard smiled. "Cousins," he said with a soft laugh. Then his expression became severe. "Kissing cousins, perhaps?"

"Perhaps," she said, feeling herself blush. But she couldn't deny the pleasure she found when his lips meekly met hers. He drew back to look into her eyes, touching her face with gentle fingers as he said, "When you do give your heart, LeNay, I pray it will not be broken by this dreadful war."

He kissed her again quickly, then gave her some semblance of a hug before he relaxed and they sat in comfortable silence. The conversation became casual again, until he insisted that it was late and they should both get some sleep. He pressed her hand briefly to his lips before he let it go, then he walked briskly away.

LeNay lay awake in her bed a long while, contemplating the time she'd spent with Richard. She was grateful for the honesty they'd shared, as much as for their tender moments. Even if he did return from the war unscathed, she doubted she would ever see him again. Still, much like his grandmother, he had left an impression on her that she would never forget.

LeNay didn't have any more time alone with Richard before he left. But as she stood with his family while good-byes were exchanged, she found it difficult not to break down and cry—the way his mother and grandmother were crying. She could see Richard putting on a brave front, looking so dashing in his uniform, but she sensed something frightened in his eyes. Considering their earlier conversations, she could almost imagine him crying his eyes out once his plane got off the ground.

Jesse's expression was completely unreadable as Richard embraced the others. But the two men clutched each other so tightly that LeNay could almost see their arms trembling as they parted. Richard turned to LeNay last, and she wondered what to say. She was surprised when he pressed a tender kiss to her lips. As he eased away, she was well aware of the astonished expressions of his family. But their surprise appeared to be pleasant—except for Jesse, who appeared downright horrified. She could well imagine him wanting to scold Richard for dallying with an outsider in this way.

"Thank you, LeNay," Richard whispered, bringing her focus entirely to him. "I will never forget you."

"Nor will I," she said. Then tears rose in her eyes as she said, "Look after yourself and be careful."

He gave her an emotional smile, then nodded firmly.

"I will," he said, "and beyond that, we'll let destiny take its course."

He gave a longing glance toward his loved ones again, then turned and walked toward the plane. He turned back once and waved, then they stood and watched the plane lift into the air. No one uttered a word while it circled around once then disappeared in the distance.

Jesse stayed for another two days, and for some reason his presence in the absence of everyone else left LeNay decidedly uncomfortable. At meals, Tyson and Lacey were paired up, as were Michael and Emma. Alexa had her grandmotherly role. And that left Jesse and LeNay. She wished that he might converse with her the way Richard had; that they could be friendly and open—if only a little. But he was so completely closed toward her that she felt as if he'd prefer that she didn't even exist, or at the very least, that she'd exist somewhere else. His arrogance angered her, but she became even more irritated with herself for actually allowing him to affect her that way. Therefore, it was an immense relief to see him leave. Along with the others she watched the plane fly away, feeling as they did that with the last of their visitors gone, the holidays were truly over.

But LeNay relished her memories of this unique Christmas. As she reread the things she'd written in her journal and added some new thoughts there, she finally focused in on what it was exactly that Alexa had given her. *Hope.* She knew now that she had been much less prepared to face the world than she'd wanted to believe. She knew that her mother's death had affected her more deeply than she'd been willing to admit, as had her father's ill treatment. She'd been frightened and unprepared to venture out on her own. And festering beneath her determination to get out and make it on her own had been a great deal of hurt and cynicism. But Alexa had restored her hope in the resilience of the human spirit. Indirectly, Alexa had taught LeNay that she could overcome the hurt and struggles of her past and find a good life. She could see the evidence that God had heard and answered her prayers, far more incredibly than she could have ever imagined. And that in itself gave her the hope to believe that he would continue to guide her through whatever the future might bring.

* * * * * * *

LeNay suddenly seemed drawn back to the present as she looked directly at Allison, saying gently, "That's what I was given for Christmas then that really meant something to me. Hope. I received many gifts from the family, but I don't remember what they were, beyond the journal. I do remember the hope, however."

The nurse came in to help LeNay into the bathroom, then she was given her medicine and brought some lunch. Allison took the opportunity to put in a new tape and set the recorder. She was actually grateful that her parents were gone, and she had this opportunity to spend this exclusive time with her grandmother. Allison ate while LeNay did, then she sat beside her again.

"Are you tired, Grandma? Would you like me to let you rest?"

"No, no. I'm quite enjoying myself."

Allison smiled. "Well, I'm glad to hear that, because I don't think I can wait to hear what happened next. I mean, I know how this story ends, Grandma. I know you ended up married to Jesse Hamilton, but you're telling me he was an arrogant snob, and you seriously disliked him."

"Well," LeNay said with a little laugh, "perspective has a way of changing." She sighed and leaned back, getting that faraway look again. "After the holidays passed, Alexa talked me into staying on. She didn't have to talk very hard. I loved it there. But she didn't have a specific job to assign me. She just asked that I help wherever I was needed. She offered to give me an allowance, you might call it, along with room and board. She was extremely generous. I did my best to find things that needed to be done . . . in the house, the yard, the garden, even in the stables, although I did my best to steer clear of the horses. They terrified me." She laughed again. "I even spent some time in the boys' home. By working that way, I got to know many different people, but I felt a little out of sorts. I didn't really belong to the family, but I didn't really belong with the hired help, either. They all had specific jobs, but I wasn't certain where I fit in. Still, I loved being there and just took it one day at a time. We knew there was a war going on, but I remember feeling that it was very far away and we were secure from its effects, beyond the minor inconveniences of having to do without certain things. There was some talk of concern for Richard, but no one seemed to want to think too hard about what might happen. We received letters occasionally; he even wrote a few to me, and of course, I wrote back.

"That winter was a mild one. Jesse came and went, never staying long. I heard talk of his education and his hobbies, but I pretended not to pay any attention. Then, about the time spring was really settling in, late September, I think, Jesse just came home one day and announced he was staying . . . for the time being. I didn't know his reasons, and I didn't care to ask. I only knew that having him around made me uncomfortable. I believe I was attracted to him, although I never would have admitted it then—not even to myself. But at the same time . . . he was an arrogant snob. It was as simple as that."

* * * * * * * *

LeNay spent the morning pulling weeds from around the vegetables in the garden, chatting easily with Rudy, the gardener. He talked mostly of the different flowers he would be planting around the house, and he seemed pleased with LeNay's offer to help.

It was past lunchtime when she returned to the house and washed up. She arrived at the dining room to find that everyone except Alexa had already eaten and left. She was sitting at the long table alone, holding a glass of lemonade and glancing through a catalog.

"Oh, hello, love," Alexa said as she looked up. "There are some sandwiches there on the sideboard. Help yourself."

"Thank you," LeNay said, still feeling at times like she should be eating in the kitchen with the servants. But Alexa always insisted that she join the family.

As LeNay sat down with a sandwich and a glass of lemonade, Alexa said, "Why don't we go sit out on the veranda and visit while you eat. It's such a beautiful day."

"That sounds nice," LeNay said, and picked up her plate to follow Alexa through French doors to the veranda that overlooked the side lawn and the stable yard.

"You know," she said, "I have many memories of sitting here with Jess."

LeNay gave her full attention to Alexa, loving the stories of her husband and the years they'd shared. Even in

Jess Davies' absence, the memories gave Alexa such obvious pleasure. LeNay became so caught up in their conversation that she was surprised to hear Alexa say, "Hello, Jesse."

"Hello, Grandma," he said just as LeNay turned to look at him. He wore his usual riding attire, along with a flat-brimmed hat that made him look all the more dashing. But he didn't even glance at her as he added simply, "LeNay."

"Jesse," she replied in the same tone, hoping he wouldn't catch her subtle effort to mimic his cool attitude.

"What are you up to today?" Alexa asked him.

"I'm going into town. Just wondered if there's anything you need."

"I don't believe so," Alexa said. "What about you, LeNay? Do you need anything?"

There were a few things LeNay wanted in town, but she wasn't about to have Jesse Hamilton get them. "No, thank you," she said more to Alexa.

Jesse walked away without another word. It seemed he could be friendly and open with Alexa, as long as LeNay wasn't around. She could almost imagine him thinking that this strange woman taken off the streets should be put with the servants where she belonged, and he wasn't about to encourage her with a smile or a kind word. It made her angry, and she wondered why she even cared.

"I worry about that boy," Alexa said after Jesse had walked away.

"Why is that?" LeNay asked.

"Well, I just keep thinking he'll grow out of it, but he doesn't."

"Out of what?"

"Why, his horrible shyness, of course."

"You mean . . . he actually knows how to say more than a dozen words?"

"Oh my, yes," Alexa laughed. "Once he gets warmed up, that boy could talk your ear right off. It's the getting him warmed up that's the problem. I've wondered endlessly why he's like that. His parents certainly aren't shy." She laughed softly. "Quite the opposite, in truth. Jesse's health wasn't good as a child. He was born premature and seemed easily prone to illness for years afterward. But then, that shouldn't necessarily make a person shy."

"I wouldn't think so," LeNay said, glancing unobtrusively toward the plane in the distance, where she could see Jesse Hamilton just now climbing in. Her heart quickened for reasons she didn't understand. *Shy?* Was it possible that this handsome, wealthy bachelor was simply helplessly shy? For some reason, the very idea suddenly made her entire perception of him change.

She watched the plane move forward and gain speed as Alexa continued. "Maybe it was all the heckling he got from having all those girls in the house—eight of them all together between his sisters and cousins. And they were all older than he was. I'm certain that's why he took so strongly to Richard, but . . . I just can't figure exactly why he's so shy."

"Maybe he just is," LeNay offered. "I had a friend in school who was terribly shy. She didn't have any problems in her life as far as I could see. I think she was just shy. It was just a part of her."

Alexa's expression became thoughtful. "I never looked at it that way," she admitted. "I believe I've spent too many years trying to figure out troubled boys in order to help them. Perhaps I've been trying to read something into Jesse that just isn't there."

"Perhaps," LeNay said noncommittally. Then she ventured to make a comment that she hoped Alexa wouldn't consider rude. "And, forgive me if I'm being presumptuous, but perhaps he would overcome it more readily if everyone around him didn't go to so much trouble to read his mind and beg his thoughts out of him."

Alexa's eyes widened. For a moment she seemed mildly alarmed, and LeNay feared she would be reprimanded, or at the very least corrected. But Alexa smiled and said, "Well, you've got quite a lot of insight, love. I think you might be right. I suppose we're all just so accustomed to doing it, we don't even think about what we're doing. And perhaps you might be able to draw him out a little as well."

"Me?" LeNay almost squeaked. "I'm absolutely certain I'm the last person on earth who could leave an impression on Jesse Hamilton." She hadn't meant to make it sound so vehement, and felt herself turn warm as Alexa seemed to be appraising her attitude.

But the older woman only smiled and said, "On the contrary." Then she said nothing more. LeNay wanted to question her on what she meant, but she already felt as if she'd exposed feelings that she didn't want anyone else looking at. If she was completely honest with herself, she couldn't deny that her lack of indifference toward Jesse Hamilton was due to attraction. But she knew it was nothing beyond a childish crush, a passing fancy—not unlike any other young woman who came in contact with him. He just had a way of leaving an impression. And if she truly had misinterpreted his shyness for arrogance, perhaps it made her attraction a little more feasible. Maybe his reticence was the very thing that drew women to him, as if he put off a silent message that he had to be conquered. Well, LeNay certainly had no intention of conquering him. But she did decide to test Alexa's theory. If his problem was simply shyness, she figured it shouldn't take much to open a door and make it comfortable enough for him to pass through. At the very least, perhaps she could satisfy her curiosity about what this man was really like.

Five
FLYING

The following day, LeNay walked the distance across the field to where Jesse's plane was parked. She found him lying beneath it, busy at something.

"Excuse me," she said, and he almost bumped his head. "Oh, I'm sorry," she added with a little laugh. "I didn't mean to startle you."

"It's all right," he said, shimmying out to where he could sit up. He stood and brushed off the back of his breeches, but he didn't say anything else. He wouldn't even look at her, and she wondered if he could really be *that* shy.

"I was just wondering if you're going into town today."

He glanced up for just a second, then looked at the ground as he said, "I wasn't planning on it, but I can if you need something."

"Oh, it's not worth a special trip. I know we need to conserve fuel, but . . . there are just a few things I need . . . when you're going. Nothing terribly important."

"Would tomorrow be all right?" he asked, still not looking up.

"That would be great," she said with enthusiasm. "I'll write down what I need . . . and get you some money, and . . ."

"Oh, the money's not a problem," he said, glancing at her again briefly.

LeNay's heart quickened. Was he actually being generous toward her?

"You're very kind," she said. "Just let me know when you're going and . . . I'll have a list ready."

"Okay," he said. "After breakfast."

"Thank you," LeNay said and walked away. She ventured to glance back once and found him watching her intently. His gaze darted away quickly with obvious embarrassment. She turned to look ahead and smiled to herself. Perhaps she *had* misjudged Jesse Hamilton.

At supper that evening, Jesse didn't so much as glance in LeNay's direction. She felt certain that even given his shyness, he simply had no interest in someone like her, and she was a fool to think otherwise. Observing him discreetly, she was amazed at how a man could look so rugged, so thoroughly masculine and mature, and at the same time appear so childlike by his expressions.

At breakfast the next morning, LeNay slid her little list across the table. "Here's what I need," she said, "if you're still going into town." Jesse took the little paper without looking up. He gazed at it for a full minute and seemed to want to say something. When he didn't, LeNay added, "I believe it's all pretty self-explanatory. Does it make sense?"

"Oh, yes," he said with a quick glance.

"Is it too much to ask?" she asked, sensing he was disconcerted over something. Then she realized she was doing the very thing that she had gently criticized Alexa for doing: prodding his words out of him with careful questions.

"No, of course not," he said.

LeNay took a deep breath and spoke firmly. "I get the feeling you're concerned about something. If you'd prefer not to bother with getting my things, it's fine. Just say so."

Through the following silence, LeNay realized everyone at the table was exchanging subtle glances of amazement and amusement. Except for Jesse, who was gaping at her as if she'd caught on fire or something. But at least he was looking at her.

"Is there something you want to say?" she asked in a gentle voice.

He glanced down, then toward his grandmother, then his parents. "I was just . . . wondering if . . . you'd want to come with me. That way, I won't . . . get the wrong thing or . . ."

LeNay was so surprised it took her a moment to gather her thoughts. "In the plane?" she asked.

"That's how I'm going," he said, nonchalantly stirring the breakfast on his plate.

"It's really quite a thrill," Alexa said, tossing LeNay a subtle wink. "I think you'd like it, love."

"I'd like that," LeNay said. "Just give me a few minutes to get ready."

She hurried upstairs to change, logically thinking that breeches would work better for getting in and out of a plane. "Oh, good heavens," she said aloud as the reality hit her with a wave of butterflies. She was actually going *flying* with Jesse Hamilton. As she walked across the field toward the plane, LeNay reminded herself that she was just an ordinary girl, lucky enough to spend some time in the middle of this family's life. If she didn't expect it to last or come to anything, then she wouldn't be disappointed. But she couldn't deny the fact that in dismissing the theory of his arrogance, she was deeply infatuated with Jesse Hamilton. And she was determined to enjoy every minute in his presence while it lasted, refusing to admit to feeling anything deeper for him.

"Hi," she said as she approached.

Jesse glanced up for a moment, showing a genuine smile toward her for the first time ever. "Hi," he said, and she felt a giddy lurch somewhere inside. "Here, put these on," he said, handing her a leather flight jacket much like the one he was wearing. It was obviously an extra of his by the way it fit her—or rather it didn't. She put the goggles on and heard him laugh, a sound that touched her deeply.

"Are you making fun of me?" she asked.

"Not at all," he said. "In my opinion, you've never looked better." He held out a gloved hand to help her in, and she felt something electric from his touch. She thought of the time she'd spent with Richard. She'd certainly enjoyed it, and she'd felt touched by his tenderness and insight. But being with him had been nothing like this.

Her heart beat quickly as she settled into the seat and watched him pull down hard on the propeller to get it started. She watched as he climbed into the plane and put on his goggles. "Are you sure this is safe?" she shouted to be heard above the engine.

He hollered over his shoulder, "I always say a prayer before I take off. I figure if I die, then God must want me to die."

"How comforting," she shouted back with light sarcasm, which made him laugh. She decided that she loved his laugh.

LeNay uttered a quick prayer, realizing he had just voiced her own theory on destiny. Then she feared that her heart would pound right through her chest as the plane moved forward, and when it finally lifted off the ground, she couldn't hold back a squeal of laughter.

"Are you having fun, or are you terrified?" he called.

"Both!" she shouted, then laughed again.

The flight was much shorter than she'd expected. Jesse helped her step down from the plane, and she enjoyed having her hand in his. But he put both hands in his pockets as they walked into town from the stretch of flat land where he'd left the plane. Their conversation consisted of him answering her questions succinctly. They got the things she needed, and he picked up a few things for himself and his mother, which he put into a black leather knapsack that he flung over one shoulder. She thought they would head back to the plane when he said, "Are you hungry?"

"Yes, actually."

"There's a place across the street that's pretty good."

They sat in silence, side by side on stools that turned. While they were waiting for the ice cream sodas and hamburgers he'd ordered, she caught his eye in the mirror behind the counter, but he looked away abruptly. LeNay searched her feelings and ventured to confront this problem once and for all.

"Jesse," she said, realizing she'd never spoken his name in his presence. She liked the way it felt on her tongue. He made a noise to indicate he was listening. She took a deep breath and just said it. "Is there a reason you won't look at me?" His face shifted toward her, and his eyes glanced at her only long enough to see that her expression was serious. He said nothing, but she sensed his nervousness and prayed that she wouldn't destroy what little progress they'd made. "I was just . . . wondering if . . . well, maybe

75

you think I'm ugly or something, and that's why you won't look at me."

LeNay was amazed by the direct gaze he gave her as he said, "No, of course not!" The tenderness in his protest disintegrated what little doubt she'd had left over him. He was decent and kind. She could feel it in his countenance. And why wouldn't he be? Everyone else related to him was.

LeNay was wondering what to say next as he turned away and sighed loudly. She was surprised when he said, "I'm just not . . . good with . . . social things. It has nothing to do with you. I'm like this with every woman. Well . . . not exactly like this."

LeNay laughed softly, unable to hold back a sudden relief. "Then I take it you haven't dated much," she said.

He chuckled and shook his head.

"Me neither," she added. "And, well . . . I'm glad to know you're just shy, because . . . I had pretty much decided that you were either an arrogant snob, or you just didn't like having me around."

Again he looked so alarmed that she couldn't help but feel touched. Their burgers and sodas were set in front of them, but he ignored the intrusion, saying somewhat brusquely, "I hope you know that's not true."

"Well, I'm beginning to see that it's not, but . . ."

When she hesitated he asked, "Did I really make you feel that way?"

"Yes," she said, and he shook his head with a grimace of self-recrimination.

"I'm sorry, LeNay, I just . . ."

"It's okay, Jesse," she said, venturing to set her hand over his for just a moment. "But . . . I would really like it if . . . you'd just . . . look at me when we talk." Worried that she might be sounding too presumptuous, she added, "Maybe you could practice on me, and then you'd feel more comfortable with other women, and . . ." She stopped when he turned his eyes slowly toward hers and held them there, gazing at her as if he'd just encountered some rare work of art. LeNay held his gaze as she put her lips over the straw of her soda, if only to keep from revealing the way his gaze affected her.

"There now," she smiled. "That wasn't so hard, was it?"

Jesse shook his head, almost seeming hesitant to draw his attention away from her to eat his burger. They ate in silence, then he paid for their food and left a generous tip. On their walk back to the plane, he said, "I'm sorry, LeNay, if I gave you the wrong impression."

She glanced up to actually find him looking at her. "It's okay," she said. "But from now on . . . maybe we could . . . be friends. If that's all right with you."

Jesse smiled and nodded, then LeNay took hold of his hand as they walked. He smiled again, which assured her that she wasn't being *too* forward. LeNay enjoyed the flight home even more, mostly since Jesse kept pointing out certain landmarks. He circled low over the station before he landed, then he helped her out of the plane. She removed the goggles but kept the jacket on as they walked toward the house. Her heart skipped a beat when Jesse Hamilton took hold of her hand. She squeezed it gently and glanced up at him with a smile that he returned easily. At the door he helped her out of the jacket and flung it over his arm.

"Thank you, Jesse. I had a good time."

"Yeah, me too," he said. "I'll see you at supper."

Once alone in her room, LeNay gave in to her urge to jump up and down with excitement. She laughed and leapt into the middle of her bed, wondering if she'd ever been so happy in her life. She only hoped that when Jesse moved on, she wouldn't end up too brokenhearted.

At supper Jesse didn't say much, but it was more than he'd said at any meal since LeNay had arrived. And he met her eyes across the table several times, often smiling at her. He excused himself before anyone else left, saying he had something to take care of. LeNay was surprised when he walked around the table and whispered close to her ear, "I'll be in the library later, if you're bored."

LeNay just nodded and watched him walk away. After the door had closed, Jesse's father said, "That's not my son. It's an impostor. I'm absolutely certain of it."

"Well, he's *my* son," Emma said, smirking toward her husband. "Perhaps he's finally found the means to overcome his shyness."

"Perhaps he has," Alexa said, setting her eyes directly on LeNay, smiling warmly.

LeNay said nothing, but she did go to the library after she'd helped wash the dishes. Jesse was sprawled out on a leather couch, engrossed in a large book spread over his lap. "Hello," she said, and he moved to stand. "Oh, don't get up. You look too comfortable." She sat on the couch beside him, but not too close. "What have you got there?" she asked, wondering if he'd wanted to show her anything in particular.

"It's my grandfather's journal," he said. "This is one of my favorite parts," he added, putting the book on her lap.

LeNay glanced at it, then looked back at him, saying, "Why don't you just tell me about it."

He hesitated, and she asked him a question about his grandfather. Within a few minutes, he was talking so freely that LeNay had trouble believing this was the same man. He lost that boyish, shy look, and she could almost literally see him evolve into a dignified, well-educated man. He was intelligent. He was funny. He was adorable. And she was madly in love with him. Even sitting here on the sofa, she felt the same sensation as being in the plane with him earlier. She felt as if she was flying.

Time flew as his stories went on. He asked her about herself, and she ended up telling him all about her mother, and the reasons she had left home following her mother's death.

During a brief lull in the conversation, he glanced at his watch and his eyes widened. "Good heavens. It's past midnight." He chuckled. "I can't believe it." Then he looked alarmed. "I'm sorry for keeping you so long. I didn't intend to—"

"It's fine," she said firmly. "I've enjoyed every minute."

LeNay felt certain she couldn't sleep after he'd walked her to the door of her room, but she actually slept quite well and went down to breakfast feeling as if she was walking on air. No, *flying*.

"Good morning, LeNay," Jesse said when she entered the dining room. He rose to help her with her chair while the others looked on in amazement. But Jesse seemed oblivious to them as he sat down and began talking to LeNay as comfortably as he had last night in the library.

During a quiet moment, Michael Hamilton rose abruptly from his chair and leaned his palms on the table, looking directly at Jesse, who appeared startled. "What have you done with my son?" Michael asked, and Jesse relaxed with a chuckle. "You've kidnaped him and taken on his identity. You're an impostor and I know it."

"I'm afraid you're the only one capable of kidnaping," Jesse said to his father, which brought out a reluctant smirk from Michael Hamilton, and the women all laughed.

Then Michael turned abruptly toward LeNay, saying firmly, *"You* must be the one who kidnaped my son and replaced him with this absolutely talkative, vibrant young man. What have you got to say for yourself?"

"Whoever this impostor may be, he's gracious and charming. And I think we should keep him around."

"Amen," Alexa said.

Michael stood up straight and sighed with mock defeat. "Very well." He pointed a finger at Jesse. "But don't be eating all the sausage."

Jesse laughed, reminding LeNay very much of his father. He turned to his mother, saying, "Where did you get him?"

"We found him on the streets," Alexa answered for her daughter.

"Brought me home like a stray puppy," Michael said, returning to his seat.

"That gives us something in common then," LeNay said.

Michael Hamilton gave her a smile that seemed to imply some hidden message. She didn't know what he was thinking, but she felt warmth radiate from him.

LeNay was the first to leave the breakfast table. She hurried to the kitchen, hoping to find some odd chore that might keep her distracted from Jesse Hamilton. After all the attention he'd given her yesterday, she feared giving him the impression that she wanted to be with him every minute— even if she did. She seemed to have urged him out of his shyness. Beyond that, the ball was in his hands. She wouldn't make a fool of herself by presuming anything.

Through the next several days, Jesse seemed to stay busy. At times he went to the boys' home with his father for hours at a time. At others, he was involved with something or other around the tracks and in the stables. But he never passed LeNay without a big smile and a warm glance. Occasionally he even winked. They spent another evening in the library, and took another flight into town. He often held her hand, but she reminded herself regularly that she had no reason to believe they were anything more than friends. She felt certain he would eventually venture out into the world again and come back with a wife. With all the progress he'd made in overcoming his shyness, she felt certain it wouldn't be too difficult for him to impress any woman. But until that happened, LeNay allowed herself to enjoy the moment and make the most of it.

One evening two weeks after her first flight into town with Jesse, LeNay sat on the veranda with a book. She'd not been there long when Jesse appeared. She looked up to see him leaning back against the veranda rail, his arms folded over his chest. Her heart skipped a beat just to see him.

"Hello," she said.

"Hi," he responded and glanced down. For the first time since she'd confronted his shyness, he appeared decidedly nervous.

"Is something wrong?" she asked.

Jesse turned his face to the side and she admired his strong profile as he said, "I need to ask you a question."

"Okay."

"If it's none of my business, LeNay, all you have to do is say so."

"Just ask," she pressed, feeling a little nervous herself.

Jesse sighed loudly. He glanced at her then looked the other direction. He cleared his throat tensely then finally said, "You . . . spent some time with Richard . . . before he left."

"Yes," LeNay said, wondering why he seemed so disconcerted. "Is there a problem with that?"

"No." He looked at her abruptly. "Of course not. Richard's a wonderful man; the best, in truth. It's just that . . ." He looked away again. "I simply have to know if . . ." She sensed him drawing courage, and saw something vulnerable in his eyes when he turned to look at her again. "Are you waiting for him, LeNay? Was there something between the two of you that—"

"No, of course not," she insisted, and his relief was so evident that LeNay's heart quickened drastically. She hardly dared believe that the implication was what she wanted it to be. Could he possibly be concerned about moving into Richard's territory if something romantic existed between them?

"But . . .," he said tentatively, "I saw him kiss you and . . ."

"It was nothing, Jesse," she said. "He made it very clear that his intentions were not romantic, and I agreed with him emphatically."

LeNay saw something in his eyes soften, which made her heart quicken further. She nearly expected him to embark on some conversation of deep importance. But he only said, "I just had to know." Then he walked away, leaving LeNay to wonder if her heart could take being around Jesse Hamilton. She found the contrast between him and Richard ironic. Richard was straightforward and communicative, not taking any chances at being misinterpreted. And Jesse could hardly get the words out to address something sensitive. Still, they were both equally good men. And she considered herself privileged to have known them at all.

The following day, LeNay wandered out to the main stables right after lunch. She was hoping to find some work to be done, but there was absolutely nobody there. She wandered between the long row of stalls, wishing she could overcome her fear of horses enough to get on one. Everybody around here made it look so easy. And she knew for a fact that a day hardly passed when Jesse didn't ride. He'd asked her more than once to go with him, but she'd managed to come up with a number of odd excuses. She wondered what it might be like to get on a horse and ride at his side.

"It's not going to bite you." Jesse's voice startled her, and he laughed when she visibly jumped.

"You never know," she said once she'd recovered. He was wearing that hat, looking absolutely stunning. His nervousness of the previous evening was completely absent.

"I figured something out about you this morning," he said, and her heart quickened fearfully as he sauntered toward her.

"And what is that?" she asked when he said nothing more.

"Whenever anything comes up about riding, or horses, you won't look at me." He touched her chin and lifted her face to his view. As he gave her a searching gaze, she concluded that he had officially overcome his shyness. "Do you have some aversion to horses, LeNay?" he asked.

She cleared her throat tensely, trying to ignore what his touch did to her. "Nothing beyond being terrified of them," she answered and he laughed. "I've never even touched a horse in my entire life."

He let go of her chin to take her hand, and the next thing she knew he was opening one of the stalls and urging her inside. She attempted to back away and he tugged gently on her arm. "Come on," he said, "she's as gentle as a lamb."

LeNay held her breath and allowed him to guide her hand down the horse's firm neck. "There now," he said. "That wasn't so hard, was it?" Their eyes met, and she recalled saying those very words to him when he'd first looked at her directly. LeNay felt suddenly unnerved by his gaze and eased out of the stall. She watched as he bridled the horse and saddled it.

"You know," he said while tightening the strap beneath the horse's belly, "we have a well-proven method of learning to ride. It even works for very young children and those unfortunate few who have never touched a horse until today."

"And what is that?" she asked, wanting desperately to learn, but at the same time wanting to run away.

Jesse said nothing. He only held out his gloved hand, as if to pose a question of trust. LeNay hesitated only a moment before she put her hand into his. He squeezed her fingers gently then bent his knee just below the stirrup, saying in a soft voice, "Put your foot there."

"Where?" she asked in a voice of panic.

"Right there," he said, slapping his thigh with his free hand. "Just put your foot there and swing your leg over the horse."

"You've got to be joking," she insisted.

"Just do it." He laughed.

LeNay took a deep breath and put her foot on his thigh, grateful to be wearing practical shoes and breeches.

She barely lifted her other leg and felt herself hoisted into the saddle while the horse remained perfectly still. She gave a little laugh of relief, then managed to say, "So, now what?"

"You just have to sit there," he said, and the next thing she knew, Jesse Hamilton was in the saddle behind her. She could hardly breathe as he put his arms around her to hold the reins. She gasped as the horse moved forward and he laughed softly just behind her ear, sending a warm shiver all through her body.

"Now just relax," he said, "and enjoy the scenery. We'll get the lesson in when we're someplace a little more private. We wouldn't want the whole station to know that this is your first time in the saddle."

"How thoughtful of you," she said, and he laughed just before he broke into a gallop. LeNay caught her breath and leaned back against Jesse's hard chest, unintentionally grabbing hold of his legs at her sides. After a few minutes she finally relaxed, relinquishing her grip. She was amazed at how beautiful their surroundings were as they rode up through the foothills. She wondered how she could have lived her entire life in Australia, and never realized how beautiful it could be.

When they came to a clearing, Jesse said, "Okay now, pay attention. Watch the reins." He showed her the basics and demonstrated them several times. Then he placed the reins in her hands, saying, "Now, you do it. The horse is well trained. She'll do whatever you tell her to do."

LeNay laughed when the horse responded so easily to her movement of the reins. Jesse coached her through turning and stopping several times, often telling her how well she was doing. "Now, see how easy that was," he said.

"I had a good teacher. But don't think I'm ready to be doing this without you in the saddle with me."

"We'll save that for our next lesson," he said, and LeNay felt butterflies at the thought of actually sharing more time with him this way.

"Take the horse over that way," he pointed, "into the trees." LeNay did as he said, and the horse ambled slowly through some trees to a place where a clear stream ran over smooth stones. "Relax the reins a little and let her drink," he said. LeNay did so and he laughed softly, sending that now-familiar chill down her back. "Very good," he drawled, and a moment later she felt his hands on her upper arms. She held her breath, wondering at his purpose. Then she didn't have to wonder as his hands moved stealthily down her arms, then back up again. The gesture couldn't possibly be misconstrued as anything but romantic. Could it? She closed her eyes, reasoning that until this moment he'd done or said nothing to indicate that they shared anything beyond a blossoming friendship. But as his hands moved lingeringly down her arms again, LeNay feared her heart might stop beating.

"You are so beautiful," he murmured behind her ear. Her breathing became sharp as she felt his face burrowing into her hair. "You even smell beautiful," he added, his voice raspy.

The silence grew long while LeNay couldn't think of any reasonable response to the way she was feeling. Jesse's grip tightened around her shoulders as he said, "You're not talking, LeNay. I've never said anything like that to a woman before. And now . . . you're scaring me."

LeNay sighed as his obvious vulnerability nearly moved her to tears. She found her voice enough to say, "I just don't understand . . . why you would say such things to me."

"Because it's true," he said. "You're the most beautiful woman I've ever seen. I've ached to be with you this way. I just can't hold it inside any longer."

"What are you saying?" she asked, attempting to turn in the saddle enough to look at him. She caught her breath as he slid down from the horse in one agile movement. With his hands at her waist, he helped her down. But even after her feet touched the ground, he didn't let go.

LeNay's hands quite naturally came to his shoulders, and she marveled at the reality of touching him this way. Jesse looked into her eyes with a deep, searching gaze, and no sign of timidity. He smiled subtly, as if he'd found what he was searching for. "LeNay," he murmured, his voice barely audible. Then his head bent, and his eyes almost closed. LeNay could hear pulse beats in her ears as she realized he was going to kiss her. Their lips barely met before he drew back only enough to look into her eyes, as if to gauge her reaction. She felt certain that her expression must have betrayed her longing when he kissed her again, meekly, slowly, a perfect balance of trepidation and yearning. LeNay instinctively moved closer and felt his arms come around her, engulfing her in an embrace of steel. He set her lips free to scatter kisses over her face. He kissed her eyelids, her earlobes, and everything in between. It was as if he'd been held back by some invisible, impenetrable wall. But now the dam had suddenly burst, allowing his feelings to finally flow through. And all this time, LeNay had never dreamed that such feelings even existed.

LeNay took his face into her hands as if she could capture this moment and hold it forever. She watched him slowly open his eyes, as if he'd just emerged from a dream. She felt in awe of the obvious adoration in his expression. But it quickly melted into concern as he murmured, "Why are you crying?"

LeNay blinked and felt tears spill over her face. "I didn't realize I was," she said, fearing the spell between them would be broken. But he closed his eyes and kissed her tears away.

"Why?" he asked again, so close to her ear that she trembled.

LeNay laughed softly and burrowed her face against his shoulder, loving the smell of his shaving lotion combined with the leather jacket he wore. "I just . . . can't believe this is happening to me."

LeNay heard him laugh softly and felt his arms tighten around her. "Funny," he said, "I was just thinking the same thing."

LeNay laughed with him, a purely delighted, giddy laugh. Jesse took a step back, as if he'd suddenly realized how close they were. "Perhaps we should get back," he said.

LeNay made no effort to hide her disappointment. "Perhaps we should, but . . ."

"But?" he asked with a sparkle of anticipation in his eyes.

"You will give me another lesson tomorrow, won't you?"

"In what?" he asked. "Riding or kissing?" He laughed and his expression became timid, as if he couldn't believe he would say something like that.

"Both," she said, touching his chin to lift his face to her view.

His expression sobered, and he kissed her once more before he mounted the horse and held a hand toward her. He gripped her arm, saying, "Get behind me."

LeNay put her foot in the stirrup and he lifted her effortlessly up. She was barely seated, with her arms around his waist, when he turned the horse and moved forward quickly. As ignorant as she was about horses, it wasn't difficult to see that his skill was incredible. She pressed her face to his back and her hands to his chest, relishing the thrill of the moment.

"You okay?" he asked over his shoulder, slowing the horse to move through some trees into a huge meadow.

"Oh, yes," she said. "It's like flying."

Jesse laughed and heeled the stallion into a gallop. LeNay felt as if she was dreaming, and prayed she would never have to wake up.

Six

JESSE'S STAR

"Hey," Jesse said as he helped LeNay down from the horse just outside the stable, "I hear there's a dance in town tonight. I usually don't go to those things, but . . . if you went with me, I might actually enjoy myself."

"I'd love to," she said, and he grinned like a child.

"We'll leave right after supper," he said and she nodded. "I need to take care of some things out here, so . . . I'll see you later."

LeNay nodded again and walked away, then she had a thought that made her turn back to ask, "Will we be flying?" He looked baffled and she added, "Into town? For the dance?"

"Uh . . . no," he said. "We'll drive."

LeNay sighed with relief. She wasn't certain how she would manage to feel presentable for a dance after flying. "Okay. I'll see you later, then." They exchanged a smile that provoked butterflies inside of her as she recalled how it had felt to be in his arms. She felt relatively certain that he was remembering too, by the way he glanced away timidly before he walked into the stable.

LeNay hurried up the stairs, so full of excitement she could hardly bear it. Then a thought occurred to her that made her stop at the landing. She didn't have anything she could possibly wear to a dance. Since she'd come here, she'd had no reason to wear anything beyond practical clothing, except for the suit she had worn on Christmas Eve. She had a couple of dresses, but Jesse had seen her in each of them dozens of times. And not one of them was suitable for such an occasion. She stood there for a few minutes, wondering what she might do, then she recalled the seemingly hundreds of times Alexa had said, "If you need anything, love, anything at all, you just have to ask."

LeNay turned around and went back downstairs to search out the places Alexa would normally be this time of day. She finally found her in the music room, toying with the piano.

"Hello," the older woman said brightly.

"Forgive me for disturbing you, but . . ."

"Oh, you're not disturbing me. Come in. What have you been up to?"

"Well," LeNay laughed softly and felt herself turn warm as she thought of the answer to that question. She settled for saying, "Jesse gave me a riding lesson."

"Oh, my," Alexa said. "It would seem he's really coming out of his shell."

"It would seem so," LeNay added, trying not to smile too much and give away her secret.

"You seem rather chipper," Alexa said, and LeNay couldn't hold back a little laugh. "I take it you enjoyed yourself."

"Very much, actually. And . . . well, he asked me to go to a dance with him this evening."

Alexa gave a delighted little laugh. "Well, it's about time."

"It is?" LeNay countered.

"What I mean is that you are very good for him, love. I'm sure you'll have a wonderful time."

"I'm sure I will, but . . . the thing is . . . Well, you told me if I ever needed anything to come to you, and . . ."

"What is it, love?" Alexa asked when she hesitated.

"I just don't know what I would wear. My clothes are so dull, and—"

"That is certainly not a problem," Alexa said, coming to her feet with an expression of pleasure. "Let's go see what we can find." LeNay followed her up the stairs. "I don't think we're shaped too differently," she said. "Perhaps what I have will be too old-fashioned for you, but—"

"Oh, no," LeNay said. "You have very good taste, in my opinion."

"You're terribly sweet, love."

"I mean it," LeNay said, following Alexa into the huge bedroom she'd shared with Jess Davies through their lifetime together. Glancing quickly around, she could feel a flavor of the man she'd heard so much about. LeNay doubted that Alexa had changed much of the decor in his absence.

"Now, let's see," Alexa said, pulling open the wardrobe to reveal a variety of dresses. "You're welcome to use anything you like."

"Oh, goodness," LeNay said, reaching out to touch the different fabrics, feeling like a child in a candy shop. While she hesitated, Alexa started pulling dresses down and holding them against LeNay. They narrowed it down to three choices, which Alexa insisted she try on. But the first one that LeNay wore felt so good that she felt no need to try the others. "It's perfect," she said, turning to view herself in the long mirror. The fabric was soft and light-weight, pale pink with darker pink flowers scattered about. The bodice was fitted, then the skirt flared out with a floaty look to it.

"You really look good," Alexa said with a soft laugh.

"It's so lovely. I doubt you could find a dress like this these days, with all the shortages of fabric."

"That's probably true," Alexa said. "Now, do you need stockings?

"No, I have good stockings. And my shoes will work."

"Jewelry?" Alexa asked.

"I don't really . . . have any. Do you think I should wear some?"

"Well, why don't we try a few things and see what works."

Alexa brought out a variety of jewelry, some pieces that LeNay realized were terribly expensive. Alexa tried different necklaces on her and settled for a gold chain with a diamond pendant, shaped like a teardrop.

"Is it a real diamond?" LeNay asked.

"It is," she said. "Jess gave it to me for one of our anniversaries."

"Oh, I can't wear this. What if I—"

"Wear it," Alexa insisted with a smile. "You're going dancing with Jess's grandson, his namesake, his pride and joy." She sighed and added with emotion in her voice, "I do believe you've got him dazzled, love."

LeNay glanced down timidly. "I don't know if I would have believed that yesterday. But today, I . . ."

"What?" Alexa asked, taking her hand.

LeNay smiled at this incredible woman who had given her so much. "Is it all right for me to admit to his grandmother that he kissed me?"

Alexa's countenance filled with a perfect contentment. "He's a good man, LeNay. I think the two of you are well suited for each other."

"You really think so?" she asked.

"As long as we're sharing secrets, perhaps I can tell you now that I thought that very thing not long after you'd recovered from that dreadful fever. I remember looking at you across the room and thinking, 'Here's a girl who might actually make a difference to Jesse.' And so it's come to that."

"Well, just because he kissed me, I wouldn't be making wedding plans or anything."

"We'll see," Alexa said. "Just enjoy each day for what it is."

"Yes," LeNay attempted to quell a rush of nerves, "I'm trying to do that. I just hope it's not too good to last."

LeNay went down to supper all ready to leave for the dance. She wore Alexa's dress and necklace, with her only pair of seamed stockings showing from the knees down, and her black shoes. In her pocket was a tube of lipstick to touch up the rich, deep pink she had put on her lips. Over her arm was a black sweater in case it got chilly. All eyes turned toward her when she entered the dining room, and she felt suddenly like a spectacle. She wondered where Jesse was as his father said, "Look at you. Is this a special occasion?"

"Actually . . . ," she said, wondering how to explain. Then she felt a hand at the small of her back, and Jesse appeared beside her.

He gave her a warm smile and an appraising gaze before he said, "Actually, she's going dancing with me."

"Lucky boy," Michael said.

"Indeed," Jesse said more softly, looking into LeNay's eyes. "You look beautiful."

"Thank you," she said, noting the dark suit he wore that made her heart miss a beat. She'd not seen him dressed this way since Christmas Eve. "You look pretty good yourself," she added, and he grinned before he escorted her to the table and helped her with her chair.

The minute they were finished eating, Jesse took her out the side door where a car was parked that she'd never seen before. She didn't know what the make was, but it just looked like something Jesse Hamilton would drive: classic.

"I don't use it often," he said, holding the door for her. "I usually fly." He walked around and got in, driving away from the house with a blatant lack of conversation. But he glanced at her occasionally, his eyes sparkling, and not the least bit timid. "You really do look nice," he said. "I'd swear that dress looks familiar, but . . ."

"It's your grandmother's," she admitted. "I didn't really have anything nice enough, but she rescued me." She touched the tear-shaped diamond. "The necklace is hers, too. She's really very good to me."

"She's that way," he said.

"I truly love her," LeNay mused. "I feel as if I've known her forever."

Jesse smiled almost mischievously. "I'd wager I could tell you something about Alexa Davies that you don't know."

"Like what?" she asked.

"Has she told you the story about Crazy?"

"What?"

"Crazy. A race horse."

"No, I don't believe I've heard about it."

"Has she told you how she met Jess Davies?"

"She was disowned in her father's will, and came to Jess for a job."

"True. But she didn't tell you what her job entailed, or you would have heard about Crazy."

"I'm listening," LeNay said.

"Jess was almost bankrupt. He was staking everything on a horse race, and he hired Alexa on the condition that she win the race by training the horse and jockey. The day of the race, the jockey got sick, and Alexa rode the race. But you have to understand, this was 1888. Women didn't wear breeches. And they certainly didn't race. But Alexa did both."

LeNay smiled at the image as he continued. "You should have heard Jess Davies tell this story. It was unforgettable."

"I can imagine," she said, wondering if Jesse Hamilton was anything like the famous Jess Davies.

"Anyway, Alexa was riding the race, but Jess didn't realize it was her. Turns out, the saddle had been rigged. About halfway through, the girth snapped and she almost fell off. But she somehow managed to get rid of the saddle and make up the lost time to win the race."

"Alexa? Really? Your grandmother?"

"Is it so difficult to imagine?"

"No, I suppose it isn't." She sighed. "She's an incredible woman. I'll be forever grateful that she took me in."

Jesse took her hand into his. "So will I." The meaning in his gaze provoked the memory of his kiss, and she turned warm.

LeNay enjoyed every minute of the dance with Jesse. Neither of them were the greatest dancers, but they managed well enough and shared a great deal of laughter in the process. The music was vibrant, and she simply loved being with him. He obviously knew many people there, but he didn't seem interested in anyone but her. LeNay was aware of a number of young women watching him and whispering, and she could well imagine their speculations. He was surely well known in the area as the wealthy bachelor. LeNay found it ironic that his wealth meant nothing to her. If she had been taken in by a family of dirt farmers, struggling to stay fed, she would have felt no less blessed.

She noticed that when people greeted him, they called him Michael. "Why is that?" she asked as he took a sip of punch from her cup.

"Officially my parents wanted me to be Michael, so that's what I've always been known by publicly. It's only at home I'm called Jesse, to keep me from getting mixed up with my father."

"Which do you prefer?" she asked.

"It doesn't matter," he said. "They are both fine names; my father and grandfather are both fine men."

"So," she smirked and took back her punch, "I can call you Michael if I feel so inclined."

"You," he said, kissing her quickly, "can call me anything you want." They shared an intense gaze, then LeNay glanced away, fearing she'd melt otherwise. She happened to notice some young women not far away, obviously quite interested in what Jesse was doing.

"I think you're being gossiped about," she said nonchalantly.

Jesse discreetly glanced the same direction, then back to her. "They're a bunch of money-grubbing bimbos," he said with such vehemence that she couldn't help laughing.

A slow song began to play and Jesse set the cup aside, escorting her purposefully onto the floor. While he held her close with an arm around her waist, he took hold of her other hand and pressed it to his shoulder. Through the entire song his eyes never left hers, even for a moment. As the music was coming to an end, she said softly, "You've overcome that afraid-to-look-at-me thing."

"Yes," he smiled, "I believe I have."

The song ended and they stopped dancing, but Jesse just held her close, apparently oblivious to their surroundings. She felt his lips come close to her ear, then he drew a breath that made her tingle even before he said, "Would it scare you away if . . . I told you that I love you?"

LeNay drew back enough to look into his eyes, searching for sincerity. And quickly finding it. While the biggest part of her felt elated and giddy, a tiny piece of logic filtered through to her tongue. "Don't tell me such things, Jesse, unless it's forever."

Jesse looked briefly startled, then he glanced around as another song began and it became far too loud to converse. He took her hand and led her briskly outside. He urged her back against the brick wall and leaned into her. His eyes were intense, and she wondered if she'd made him angry. Did he believe she was questioning his sincerity? He took her shoulders into his hands, and with no warning, pressed his mouth over hers. Their kiss turned warm and moist, with no sign of anger. Her arms went up over his shoulders by their own will, and their lips parted only long enough for him to say, "Forever isn't long enough."

Jesse finally stepped back, and she could almost feel his conscious effort to maintain proper boundaries between them. "Do you want to dance any more?" he asked.

LeNay shook her head, knowing that last dance couldn't be topped. "My feet are killing me," she said and he took her hand, leading her toward the car.

"Wait," she said before he opened the door for her. "Do you have a handkerchief?"

He dug in his pocket and produced one, monogrammed with JMH, she noticed. She took it from him and he smiled when she began rubbing lipstick off from around his mouth. "I think this color looks better on me," she said. He helped her into the car, then walked around to get in while she touched up her lips in the rearview mirror. He watched her and smiled as she put the lid on the tube and tucked it into her pocket. Then he closed the door and the dome light turned off.

The silence became filled with tension as they drove, and LeNay wondered why. She decided to approach it head-on. "Did I do something wrong?"

He looked at her in surprise, then turned back to the road. "No," he said in a gentle voice. "I'm afraid you do everything just right."

"You're afraid?" she asked. He said nothing. "You're not talking, Jesse. I won't try to read your mind."

"I don't know what to say."

"Just say what you're thinking."

He laughed briefly, then rubbed a hand over his face. He was visibly nervous. "My dear LeNay, if I told you even a little bit of what I've been thinking, I'm afraid the entire contents of my mind would just spill all over the ground. And if that happens, I'm afraid I'll just . . . scare you away. And that's what frightens me most of all."

LeNay's heart quickened as she read between the lines. *What was he trying to say?* Intuitively she reached her hand across the seat and took his. "Jesse," she said, "what makes you think that you would scare me away?"

"Because," he said with that nervous laugh again, "if *you* said such things to *me,* I would probably run."

It took LeNay a full minute to perceive what he was saying. She thought through her response carefully. "I can't promise how I'll respond to your thoughts, Jesse, because I don't know what they are. But I don't believe there's anything you could say that would frighten me, if it came from the heart. And . . . well . . . maybe you should know . . . the only thing that really frightens me is . . ."

"What?" he urged gently, squeezing her hand.

"I fear that this magic spell you have woven around me . . . I fear it will end."

Jesse gazed at her as long as he could without losing sight of the road ahead. She sensed his surprise and perhaps . . . concern. But he said nothing for several miles. He finally broke the silence by saying, "I have a question."

"All right."

"Is it necessary for you to sit all the way over there?"

LeNay let out a little laugh of relief and sidled up next to him as he put his arm around her shoulders. She quickly relaxed and was surprised to feel the car come to a stop.

"I must have dozed off," she said as he turned off the engine.

She felt a kiss on the top of her head before he asked, "Do you think those aching feet of yours could bear a little walk in the moonlight?"

"If I take off my shoes, I could bear just about anything."

Jesse laughed and opened the door. He got out and motioned her toward him. She was almost out of the car when he went down on one knee and lifted her foot into his lap. The yard between the house and the stables was well illuminated by the electric lights, making it possible to see his boyish grin before he bent his head to concentrate on unfastening the little buckle around her ankle. He removed both her shoes then helped her to her feet, tossing the shoes into the car.

"Wait," she said, recalling that she had stockings on. "Nylons are too precious to wear out by walking around in them." She glanced around to be assured they were completely alone, then she turned her back to him. "Don't peek," she said and lifted her skirt enough to unfasten her garters and roll the stockings down her legs. She tossed them into the car with her shoes, and he closed the car door. With his arm around her shoulders they moved away from the house, walking toward the field where his plane was parked. A half moon lit the night enough to see clearly where they were going. LeNay felt suddenly chilled and stopped.

"Is something wrong?" he asked.

"I left my sweater in the car. Let me go back and . . ."

Jesse removed his jacket and put it around her shoulders. "Will this work?"

"Perfectly," she said. They walked a little farther, while it became evident that he had a destination in mind. But he didn't appear to be heading directly to the plane. He stopped and looked one direction, then he turned and looked another. He took several steps with her hand in his, then he did it again.

"This is the place," he declared.

"What do you mean?" she asked with a laugh.

Jesse pointed to the mountains in the distance. "When I stand in this spot, that peak is directly northwest. And if I turn exactly ninety degrees this way," he demonstrated, "then the center gable on the boys' home is directly northeast. And if I stand in this spot and look directly . . ." He pointed and turned. "That way . . . considering the time of year and the time of day. There. That's Richard's star."

"I don't understand."

"I was still a boy when Richard left home the first time. He was my hero." Jesse chuckled. "He still is, I suppose. I was devastated to think of being without him. But he brought me out here, and he showed me what he called his favorite star. I don't remember its name exactly. I've always called it Richard's star. But he told me it was the star he would follow to guide him home, and that no matter where he went, I could look at his star and remember that his heart was with me."

"How sweet," LeNay said, gazing at the specified star. Her memories of Richard made the thought all the more tender. "So . . . why this spot in the field? Can't you find the star standing anywhere?"

"Of course. But this is the very spot where I would lie for hours as a child, waiting for his plane to come in. I don't remember why I picked this spot initially; some childhood game, I suppose. I had a very vivid imagination."

He sat down on the ground and LeNay sat beside him, pulling her legs up beneath the ample fabric of her skirt. Looking upward, she asked, "So, where's Jesse's star?"

"I don't have one."

"How about . . ." She looked around. "That one."

"No," he said, his tone becoming severe, "I think my star is right here." He touched her chin and looked into her eyes, moving closer. "You are everything I need to find my way home."

LeNay took a deep breath and repeated her admonition of earlier, at the risk of making a tense moment even more tense. "Don't say such things to me, Jesse, unless it's for—"

"It *is* forever," he interrupted, taking hold of her arms. "I love you, LeNay. I think I loved you the first time I saw you. But I couldn't tell you how I felt when I couldn't even look at you. And then when I—"

"Wait a minute," LeNay said once she'd digested the fact that Jesse Hamilton had just told her he loved her. "The first time you saw me? That was Christmas Eve, when you were walking toward the house."

"That's right," he said. "I remember it like it was yesterday."

LeNay pressed a hand over her middle to quell an inner trembling as she tried to perceive what that meant. All these months as he came and went, hardly even acknowledging her. Was it possible that he'd really felt this way all along? While she was trying to make sense of it, he went on in a timid voice.

"I've always been shy, LeNay. And I was always worse around women. But when I was anywhere near you, I'd just freeze. Somehow I just knew that if I actually said something to you, I'd certainly muff it up. And then when I saw the way Richard behaved toward you, I wondered how I could bear actually seeing you become involved with *him,* of all people. While I was away from home, I found myself thinking of you constantly. I came home to stay because I was afraid you'd leave and I'd never find you again. I knew I'd never get to know you if I didn't stay around for more than a few days at a time. But I felt certain you hated me, although I couldn't figure why. And then when you started talking to me, I could hardly believe it. When you told me that I'd given you the impression I didn't like you, I actually felt sick inside. And then, when you told me there was nothing between you and Richard, I was so relieved I could hardly bear it. Do you hear what I'm saying, LeNay?"

"Very clearly," she murmured, recalling his words in the car. . . .*If I told you even a little bit of what I've been thinking, I'm afraid the entire contents of my mind would just spill all over the ground.*

"Have I scared you yet?" he asked and she shook her head, fearing she would cry if she tried to talk. "You're not saying much," he added.

"I don't know what to say."

"When *I* said that," Jesse countered, *"you* told *me* to just say what I was thinking."

LeNay looked up at him, marveling at the sincere vulnerability in his eyes as much as the things he'd said. She forced her voice past the emotion, hearing it crack as she said, "I think that . . . I've never heard anyone say anything so completely incredible in my life." She felt his sigh of relief brush her face. And she went on, knowing it was her turn to spill her thoughts. "I didn't want to love you. I didn't even want to *like* you. Everyone else loved you so much . . . Everyone wanted to be around you. Even the servant girls. They'd talk about you, speculating and giggling."

"They did?" he said with such perfect innocence that LeNay laughed and took hold of his arms, pressing the side of her face to his shoulder to hide her tears.

"I convinced myself you were arrogant and rude; a spoiled rich boy with too much money and too much attention. But I was wrong, Jesse; so completely wrong. I love you, Jesse Michael Hamilton."

She heard him laugh and felt his arms around her, holding her close. Then he lifted her chin to look into her eyes. "Don't say such things to me, LeNay, unless it's forever."

They laughed together, and then he kissed her. And kissed her. It was even more wonderful than she'd remembered. He caressed her hair and kissed her face, not leaving any part of it untouched. He traced his finger over the gold chain encircling her neck, and fondled the diamond pendant while his lips explored her throat, provoking a tingling unlike anything LeNay had ever felt.

He found her mouth again and kissed her as if he never had before. In the midst of it he laughed and she pulled away. "What's so funny?"

"Nothing's funny, LeNay. I just can't believe it. I never dreamed I could be this happy; that I could feel what you make me feel."

"I could agree with that," she said, wanting him to kiss her again, but knowing they needed to be careful. Jesse lay back in the grass and pointed upward. "I think that's LeNay's star."

"Which one?" she asked, lying beside him with her head on his shoulder.

"It doesn't matter." He laughed. "Any star in the sky will do." He turned to look at her face. "They all lead me back to you."

"Oh, so you're a poet?" she said with a giggle.

"I guess I am now." He laughed. "Jess Davies was a poet."

"Really?"

"Oh, yes."

"Do you know any of his work?"

"Only one, at least enough to recite it."

"Oh, I want to hear," she said eagerly.

Jesse cleared his throat dramatically, then he laughed. "Okay, here goes," he said. "It's called *Alexa.*"

"Really?"

"Really. Now hush up and listen."

"I'm listening," LeNay said, settling deeper against his shoulder, marveling at the sky above her as he spoke in a voice that seemed deeper and more raspy than usual. She could almost imagine the shy Jesse Hamilton, reciting his grandfather's poetry aloud as he flew alone in the heavens.

"There stands a man and in his hands
    he holds elusive dreams
Like shooting stars and shimmering sands
    they fall and roll to sea
He felt them slipping from his grasp
    and falling to the ground
But Alexa came and picked them up
    and turned his dreams around
Alexa with her wild eyes,
    those eyes that stir my soul
She picks the little pieces up,
    like new, she makes them whole
Alexa, now I bare my soul
    and leave it in your hands

Please hold it gently with the dreams,
  the shooting stars and shimmering sands."

"That's incredible," LeNay said softly, then silence surrounded them.

She realized she'd dozed off when she heard Jesse say, "We should get back. I suspect it's the middle of the night."

LeNay only nuzzled closer to him. A minute later she heard him say, "I'll be right back." She felt suddenly chilled without his warmth beside her. But a moment later she felt a blanket come over her and heard him whisper, "I always keep a couple in the plane. Go back to sleep."

Once LeNay felt his shoulder beneath her head again, she did just that.

Seven
CASUALTIES OF WAR

LeNay opened her eyes and squinted from the sunlight. Then she turned to see Jesse leaning on one elbow, watching her intently. He smiled. He touched her face. He kissed her.

"If I'm dreaming, don't wake me," she murmured and stretched.

"You're wide awake, my love," he said, and she laughed.

"I'm the most fortunate woman alive."

"How is that?"

"Jesse Michael Hamilton just called me his love."

He chuckled and kissed her again. "I think we missed breakfast. He jumped to his feet and took up the blanket covering her, throwing it over his shoulder. Then he took both her hands into his and pulled her up. She'd barely come to her feet when he lifted her into his arms, making her giggle.

"I think I could manage to walk myself," she said.

"But this is much more fun."

When they were almost to the house, he started to run and she squealed with laughter. He stopped running and turned in circles while she threw her head back, shouting toward the sky, "I'm flying!"

Jesse laughed, then stopped suddenly. "Wait," he said, and set her feet down, taking hold of her waist. "Now, wrap your legs around me."

"What?" she gasped, and he laughed.

"It's nothing scandalous. It's just a flying lesson."

LeNay remembered the children wrapping their legs around Jesse's waist as he'd twirl them around. She felt briefly hesitant, knowing she weighed more than even his oldest nephew. "Trust me," he said gently. "I won't let you fall."

LeNay took a deep breath. She put her hands at his shoulders and jumped as he lifted her up. She was grateful for the full skirt as she wrapped her legs around his waist. With his hands pressed to her back, he said, "Now let go, and put your arms out." LeNay took another deep breath and leaned back against his hands. He immediately turned around and she squealed with laughter, feeling a weightless sensation that made her breathless and jittery—and dizzy.

Jesse laughed as he stopped and teetered a little. "There, now you've had a flying lesson," he said. Then he shifted her in his arms, cradling her against him as if he could hold her there forever. He moved on toward the house, then they noticed Jesse's parents sitting on the veranda, holding hands. Michael's booted legs were propped on an extra chair, crossed at the ankles. By their expressions, they had obviously observed the antics going on. Jesse stopped walking, but he didn't put her down.

"That's quite a ruckus you're making," Michael said with a little upward twitch of his lips.

"That's quite a dance you must have gone to," Emma added, smiling as subtly as her husband had.

With a perfectly straight face, Jesse said, "We slept together in the field."

LeNay hit him but couldn't help laughing when he did. She noticed his parents exchanging a glance, but their expressions didn't change. "We are both perfectly chaste, I can assure you," LeNay said, wiggling out of Jesse's arms to stand beside him, recalling that she was without shoes.

"I should hope so," Emma said.

While LeNay was digesting the fact that Jesse Hamilton had inherited some of his father's wry sense of humor, he put an arm around her and said firmly, "We're getting married."

LeNay turned to him in astonishment, wondering if this was meant to be part of his humorous antics. But his expression was perfectly serious. "You haven't even asked me, Jesse Michael Hamilton. Don't go thinking that—"

"Will you marry me?" he asked. LeNay glanced at his parents to find them still watching, seeming subtly amused. Then she looked back to Jesse and reminded herself to stop gaping. The intensity of his eyes deepened as he added, "Well?"

"Oh come on, boy," Michael drawled. "You can do better than that. I wouldn't answer you either, if that's the best you can do."

"Well, I don't want to marry *you*," Jesse said to his father.

"I should hope not," Emma said, moving a little closer to her husband. "But take it from me, Jesse, your father has a way with women. I'd listen to him if I were you."

Michael stood up and motioned with one finger for Jesse to come closer. He left LeNay standing where she was and ran up the steps to the veranda. Her heart quickened as she watched Michael whispering in his son's ear. Jesse smiled. He chuckled and nodded his head. Then he jumped over the veranda rail and approached her, abruptly going down on one knee and taking her hand into his.

"LeNay," he said with such intensity in his eyes that she almost felt moved to tears, "you've made me realize that I couldn't possibly live without you. I'm asking you to marry me, from the heart. And I pledge myself to you, heart and soul."

LeNay didn't think anything could be more embarrassing than getting a marriage proposal in front of the would-be groom's parents. But then tears trickled down her face to prove her wrong. "Of course I'll marry you," she managed to say, trying to ignore the fact that Emma was crying, too.

Jesse gave a little laugh and came to his feet, then with no warning, he took her into his arms and kissed her, long and tender. He eased back with a warm chuckle, wiping her tears away with his fingers, and she realized that he actually had the glisten of moisture in his eyes. He blinked it back and kissed her again. With his arms around her, he turned toward his parents, saying lightly, "How was that?"

"Much better," Michael said. Then he nudged Emma and added, "He's such a good boy." He laughed, then motioned with his arm. "Get up here. Both of you."

Jesse and LeNay walked up the steps, where Michael and Emma met them with embraces. "We couldn't be happier," Emma said. "But I think you'd better go inside and tell your grandmother."

"And then some breakfast might be good," Michael said. "If there's any left."

Jesse took LeNay's hand and led her into the house. Once inside the door, she tugged on his hand to stop him.

"What?" he said, turning to look at her. Suddenly overcome with emotion, LeNay couldn't speak. Jesse chuckled tenderly and wiped at her tears. "Why are you crying?" he asked.

"I just . . . can't believe it. Ever since I've come here, I've felt as if I was somehow living in a dream, and I've dreaded the day when I might actually have to leave. And now . . . everything has changed in the course of a day, and I . . ." She sniffled and pressed her face to his shoulder.

"And now you'll never have to leave," he said, and she felt his lips in her hair.

"I love you, Jesse," she murmured, holding him close. "I must be the most fortunate woman alive."

"You mentioned that earlier," he said, looking into her eyes. "But I am the fortunate one." He gave her a long, slow kiss, then took her hand again. "Come along. Let's find Grandma. I don't think she'll be terribly surprised. I suspect she's been doing a little undercover matchmaking."

LeNay chuckled. "Only because she has good instincts."

"She does indeed," he said, and pushed open the door to the music room to find Alexa sitting by the window with a cup of coffee.

"Well, good morning," Alexa said, then she looked them over and smiled slightly. "Isn't that what you were wearing when you left here last night?"

"Yes, actually," Jesse said. "We had a lot to talk about."

Alexa took in their clasped hands and LeNay's bare feet. "I take it your talk went well."

"Yes, actually," Jesse said again. "We wanted you to be one of the first to know that . . . well," he smiled toward LeNay, "we're getting married."

Alexa didn't appear surprised, but her pleasure was readily evident as she stood and embraced them both at the same time. "Oh, it's simply incredible," she said. "When two wonderful people come together, good things are bound to happen."

They talked for a while with Alexa, then they went to the dining room to find that all evidence of breakfast had been cleared away. "I guess we'll have to wait until lunch," he said.

"I don't think so," LeNay countered and led him to the kitchen. They found it presently unoccupied, and LeNay found some bread and a couple of apples, then she began digging in the ice box where she found some cheese, and some cold ham left from the previous evening's supper. She also pulled out some butter and milk, arranged everything on a tray, and handed it to Jesse.

"You're very resourceful," he said with a laugh.

"To the dining room, my love. We shall have our own breakfast."

Jesse headed toward the door, then LeNay turned back to get a jar of jam. She heard him say, "Hello, girls," followed by a chorus of childish giggles.

LeNay held back and observed, wondering if Jesse had ever said anything directly to Rita and Jill before. It was evident that he'd overcome his shyness with others as well. She could see them gushing and beaming, but she found it suddenly terribly amusing. "Here, let me take that for you," Rita said.

"Oh, it's all right," Jesse said. "I was just going to the dining room to—"

"I'll take it," Jill insisted. She took it from his hands before he could protest, and they both moved into the hall.

Jesse glanced toward LeNay with a look that combined bewilderment with a little disgust, but she grinned and motioned for him to follow the girls. She stayed a few steps behind, and hesitated in the doorway of the dining room as the tray was set on the table and they both looked at Jesse as if they might fall at his feet.

"Is there anything else you need?" Rita asked.

"Uh . . . no, I don't believe so." He glanced toward LeNay, who comically held up the jar of jam, but Rita and Jill had their backs turned to her and didn't notice.

"I was thinking that some jam might be nice, but . . . ," he motioned toward the door, "it looks as if LeNay's already got it."

Both girls turned toward LeNay with obvious disappointment in their eyes. She wondered if they had noticed Jesse's attention toward her, but she couldn't recall either of them ever being around when they'd been together. They both hovered in the room, saying nothing, but apparently not wanting to leave. Jesse cleared his throat gently and said, "I believe we have all we need. LeNay and I are going to eat now."

They both nodded and skulked away. Jesse shook his head and LeNay chuckled. "You're breaking their hearts," she said. "You finally start speaking to them, then you make it clear you intend to dine with *me.*"

"I'm certain they'll get over it," he said, helping her with a chair. They were barely seated when she said, "I forgot some silver. We have nothing to butter the bread with or—"

"I'll get it," he said, but she stood up and hurried toward the door.

"No, it's okay. I know right where it is."

LeNay walked into the kitchen and realized that Jill and Rita were talking about her rather unfavorably. She caught her name and the words . . . *gold digger, manipulating Mrs. Davies and moving in on . . .*

They both looked up with wide eyes when LeNay entered the kitchen. She fought the burning between her eyes and reminded herself to behave with dignity. "I'll just be a second," she said and pulled open a drawer to retrieve what she needed. But as she turned to leave the room, hot tears burned into her eyes and she moved blindly out the door, praying they wouldn't notice. She bumped directly into Jesse, who said, "I wanted some coffee. I'll just . . ." He noticed her expression and took hold of her shoulders. "What's wrong?" he asked.

"Nothing," she murmured, but he glanced over her head toward Jill and Rita. Then the reticent Jesse Hamilton took a step past her and stated resolutely, "In the future, if you have anything to say about my fiancée, you will discuss it with me. I'll not have gossiping in the kitchen. Any more of this and Mrs. Davies will hear about it." His voice didn't hold a trace of malice or anger; it was as firm and composed as his manner. He added in the same tone, "We would like some coffee in the dining room."

He took LeNay's arm and led her away. "How did you know?" she asked, trying to get hold of herself.

"I was right behind you. I heard what they said."

"And how do you know it's not true?" she asked, refusing to wonder if a part of him had believed what he'd heard.

"I just know," he said, his voice tight.

"How do you know?" she demanded. "How can you be certain I'm not after the money and prestige, just like the rest of them?"

Jesse stopped just inside the dining room and turned her to face him. "Because I *know*," he growled. "Because I feel it right here." He pressed a fist to his chest. "First of all, my grandmother is not that stupid. She would not open her heart and home to *anyone* if she had any minuscule reason to believe that their motives for being with her were not pure. She is discerning and wise, and her instincts are good. And for myself, I may have trouble talking to people, but I don't have any trouble observing them. I saw your true character in your eyes a long time ago. And that's when I started looking beyond the fact that I was madly in love with you, and realized that I could actually *love* you."

"And when was that?" she asked, her tears turning to a soft laugh of relief.

Jesse sighed. "Christmas Eve," he said. "At the boys' home. I could hardly keep my eyes off you. Your humility and awe were so apparent. And then," he chuckled, "I was walking back to the house right behind you, and you were carrying your shoes. All things combined, I was sunk from that moment."

"I love you, Jesse," she said.

"Yes, I know you do. And that's why I asked you to marry me. Nothing else matters." He bent to kiss her, and LeNay forgot that she was hungry. He pulled her so close that she could hardly breathe, at the same time wanting only to be closer.

Their kiss broke apart when they heard a sharp gasp. They both turned at the same time to see Rita with a coffee tray.

"Thank you," Jesse said. When she didn't move he added, "You can set it there." She did so and scurried out of the room. Then Jesse kissed her again.

117

After sharing their haphazard breakfast, Jesse escorted LeNay to her room, where he left her with another kiss. He told her he had some things he needed to do with his father in the boys' home as soon as he changed his clothes. LeNay felt disoriented without him, but she got cleaned up and put on fresh clothes before going out to help Rudy in the garden. She missed lunch, since she was still plenty full from her late breakfast, and she knew Jesse wouldn't be there. Late in the afternoon she went to her room and lay down, realizing she hadn't gotten much sleep the night before. And the rest she'd gotten out in the field hadn't been terribly comfortable. Still, she laughed to herself to recall how wonderful it had been.

A knock at the door startled her from sleep. "Come in," she called groggily, thinking it was likely Alexa. After she heard the door open and close, she turned her head and was surprised to see Jesse, his hands behind his back. The reality of seeing him here in her room made her heart quicken. *He was going to be her husband.* She doubted that anything in life could make her happier.

"Napping, eh?" he said with a little smirk, moving toward her.

"Yes, but sleeping was much more pleasant when you were next to me."

"That could be arranged," he said and she laughed, wondering where his shyness had gone.

"All you have to do is marry me, Mr. Hamilton, and you can sleep with me any time you want."

He made a noise of pleasure and stood beside the bed, looking down at her with adoration in his eyes. "You know," he said, "having my father get into my car and find these was not a problem." He held up her shoes, dangling them from one hand by the ankle straps. "But when he found

118

these," he held up her stockings and she groaned, covering her face with her hands, "it was a bit embarrassing."

"I'm sorry," she said.

"I'm not." He tossed the shoes and stockings on the floor and sat on the edge of the bed. "He just grinned and told me to mind my manners. I assured him that I was not the rogue he had been at my age."

"Was he a rogue?"

"Oh, was he!" Jesse laughed. "I would have thought you'd heard that story by now."

"I'm afraid not. Tell me."

"Well, to begin with, my father was brought here as a boy, pulled off the streets. He was living on his own and stealing to survive."

"Really?" LeNay found it difficult to believe. He'd mentioned being brought here like a stray puppy, but she never would have dreamed that his circumstances might have been so dreadful.

"Apparently his parents were more horrible than you could possibly imagine. Anyway, he grew up here, then worked in the stables after he graduated. As he tells it, he was desperately in love with Emma Davies and didn't want to leave. But he finally did when something happened that made him certain she would have nothing to do with him. Four years later he came back, and—"

"And they fell in love," LeNay said, seeing the obvious.

"It wasn't quite that easy," he chuckled. "He came back and kidnaped her . . . for ransom."

"You're teasing me," she said dubiously.

"It's absolutely true." Jesse's tone was as severe as his eyes. "He kidnaped both her and Lacey. Tyson and my grandfather had to go into the outback to get them. But when all was said and done, my parents came back to announce their plans to be married."

"He *is* a rogue," LeNay declared.

Jesse lifted his brows mischievously. "Maybe I'm more like him than you think." Then with no warning, he started tickling her. He laughed while she squealed and wiggled, hitting him and begging him to stop. When he finally did, he was lying beside her, looking down into her face. He took a deep breath and kissed her with a trace of passion.

"We must be careful," LeNay murmured as feelings came to life in her that she'd never known existed until Jesse had taken her in his arms just yesterday.

"We must get married," he said close to her ear. "Very soon, I think."

LeNay laughed softly at the thought, then they went down to supper.

"We missed our riding lesson," he said on their way down the stairs. "How about tomorrow after breakfast?"

"Sounds delightful."

"I told my father and Tyson that I needed some time off." He smirked, reminding her of his father. "I told them I was courting a beautiful woman and needed to do it properly."

LeNay smiled and silently counted her blessings.

The following morning, she was relieved when Jesse got into the saddle with her rather than putting her on her own horse. Not only did she feel totally unprepared to handle a horse alone, she relished having him so near. He allowed her to take the reins as they rode the better part of the morning, and she could hardly believe how comfortable she was beginning to feel with him. When they came to the same spot where he'd first expressed his feelings, only two days ago, he dismounted and tethered the horse before he helped her down. Then he took some rather large saddlebags and a blanket off the horse that she hadn't even noticed. He flung them over his shoulder and took her hand. They walked a short distance, then he spread out the blanket and sat on it.

"Is this how you teach young ladies to ride?" she asked.

"No," he smiled, "this is how I do a picnic."

"Really?" she asked, and he pulled everything they needed out of the saddlebags.

"I must confess," he said, "that it was my mother's idea. She prepared the food."

"Your mother is very sweet."

"Yes, she is. And so are you."

They ate together, intermittently talking and laughing. The more LeNay got to know him, the more she marveled at his integrity, his depth, his sensitivity. When they were both full, he lay down with his head in her lap, and she reclined against the saddlebags. When he rolled over and woke her up, he murmured with a chuckle, "Now we've slept together on the mountain."

The following morning, LeNay ironed the freshly washed dress Alexa had let her borrow, enjoying her memories of wearing it as she did. She took it to Alexa's room to return it before breakfast, but Alexa refused to take it. "You've got some very special memories in this dress, I believe. And I haven't worn it for years. I want you to have it." Alexa thwarted LeNay's efforts to protest, but LeNay couldn't deny her thrill at being given such a wonderful gift. As she hung it in her own closet, the memories warmed her once again.

Later that morning, LeNay walked out to the clothesline behind the house to take down the laundry. It was one of many tasks she had helped with dozens of times. But this was one of her favorites, especially on the days when the housekeeper had washed the sheets, as she'd done today. The hot breeze whipped them like the sails of a ship as she took them down and folded them the way her mother had taught her. She was taking down the last one when Jesse took hold of her from behind and made her scream. "Don't sneak up on me like that!" she scolded, but he just laughed.

"It's time for a flying lesson," he said, lifting her into his arms. With little urging she wrapped her legs around his waist, and he efficiently twirled her around. Their laughter floated skyward together, and she felt certain that heaven must be close by.

After he carried the laundry basket into the house for her, he took her out to the plane and they went for what he called a *joy ride*. He flew over mountains, showing her breathtaking views. And he quickly discovered that tipping the wings to one side would make her squeal with frightened laughter. After they returned, he helped her step out onto the wing then lifted her down as he kissed her. She kissed him back, then broke away, saying, "Last one to the house gets to—"

"What?" he asked, grabbing her around the waist.

"You'll see when you get there," she said with a laugh, hoping she'd think of something before he did.

"Okay, but first a flying lesson." He twirled her around, and she decided she loved this little ritual of his. When he set her down she broke into a run and laughed over her shoulder to see him quickly gaining on her. She felt certain he was purposely holding back to allow her to win when she hurried through the door and up the stairs, hearing him close behind her, laughing with the same delight that she felt.

In a split second, everything changed. His laughter turned to a groan, and she heard a thud behind her. She turned around, heart pounding, to see him kneeling on one of the steps, both hands pressed to his chest. His breath came in spurts as he sat on the step and leaned against the wall, obviously in pain.

"Jesse!" She knelt in front of him, taking his shoulders into her hands. "What is it? What's wrong?" When he apparently couldn't answer she said, "I'm going for help. I'll be right—"

"No!" he said. "It's okay. I'll . . . be okay . . . in a few minutes."

"Has this happened before?" she asked, wishing her heart would slow down as she contemplated what might be wrong.

He nodded firmly, and she could see him making a conscious effort to slow down his breathing. She waited patiently for him to recover, and gradually he relaxed, eventually taking his hands from over his chest, as if he finally dared set it free.

"What is it, Jesse?" she asked with caution, wondering if she wanted to know.

"It's nothing to be concerned about," he said casually, but she felt hesitant to believe him. "It happened occasionally when I was a kid. The doctor told me to be careful and not exert myself too much. But it hasn't happened for years. I honestly thought I'd outgrown it."

"Are you certain it's okay?" she asked, touching his face.

123

"Yes, of course." He smiled and pulled her to him. "And don't be telling my mother and grandmother and get them all worried. I'm fine. I just need to take life a little slower, I think."

"No more flying lessons," she said.

"I'm not taking it *that* slow," he insisted with a little laugh. "But next time, I'll walk to the house."

"Okay," she said and pressed her head to his shoulder. "Be careful, Jesse. I need you."

"I need you, too," he said and kissed her.

LeNay quickly forgot about the incident when every minute with Jesse was like heaven itself. He was obviously strong and healthy, and whatever the problem might be, she had no reason to believe it would ever be a concern as long as he was careful.

Only a few days after Jesse's proposal of marriage, they returned from a riding lesson to find the family on the veranda having sandwiches and lemonade. After they had washed up, Jesse bragged about how LeNay was handling her own mount. They helped themselves to the food and sat close together. The conversation turned to wedding plans, and LeNay bubbled with excitement to hear it discussed so openly—especially when Jesse suggested they get married before Christmas. Thinking of how she'd come here just before Christmas last year, she could hardly believe the changes in her life.

Long after they finished eating, the conversation went on. Alexa talked about having LeNay wear her wedding gown, just as Emma and Lacey had done. Lacey and Emma talked of how they had all been married in the upstairs hall of the house, and Jesse and LeNay should do the same. Michael and Tyson even had their input as they all discussed the food, the champagne, the flowers. Jesse held her hand possessively in his, smiling at her often.

The conversation came to an abrupt halt when an official-looking car came around the house and parked at the end of the drive.

"I wonder who that could be," Alexa said in a tone that sent a shiver down LeNay's back. A quick glance told her she wasn't the only one who had felt it. The silence became eerie as an official-looking man got out of the car and walked slowly across the lawn toward the veranda where they were sitting, holding an envelope in his hand. Everything seemed to go in slow motion. LeNay noticed that Alexa put a hand over her heart, Lacey put both hands to her face, Emma pressed her fingers over her mouth. The three men stood in unison as the visitor approached the veranda rail, tucking his hat beneath his arm.

"I'm looking for Mr. Davies," he said in a solemn voice.

LeNay saw Tyson's expression falter for only a second before he lifted his chin in a courageous gesture, saying, "That's me."

Only then did LeNay perceive what the others had already guessed. She reached for Jesse's hand and stood beside him, startled by his painful grip when his expression was so unreadable.

"Telegram for you," the man said, and Tyson reached over the rail to take it. "I'm truly sorry," the man added. He nodded gravely and turned away.

While Tyson stared at the envelope in his hands, then glanced at each of his loved ones, the man got in his car and drove away. LeNay wondered for a moment what it might be like to have the job of delivering death notices.

Lacey stood next to her husband, and he put his arm tightly around her.

"I can't open it," Tyson said, extending the envelope toward Michael. "You read it."

Michael didn't look pleased with the assignment, but he took the envelope and opened it with trembling fingers. They all watched as his eyes scanned the contents of the page in his hands, then he looked directly at Tyson and Lacey as he said, "His plane was shot down. He's missing. They're doing everything they can to locate him, but they're relatively certain that . . . he's dead."

Time, which had seemed to be moving so slowly, suddenly raced to catch up with itself. Tyson and Lacey visibly crumbled in each other's arms. Emma clung to Michael. Alexa pressed her face into her hands. Jesse seemed frozen, unable to move or respond. LeNay felt helpless and suddenly alone. She'd barely become acquainted with Richard when he'd come home for Christmas last year, but their time together had been something tender and precious in her memory. It had been easy to care for him, even though she hardly knew him. She couldn't mourn his loss the way the others could, but she had grown to love these people who loved him dearly. She'd lived through death and she certainly understood how deeply it could wound, but she felt helpless to even respond. There was nothing she could say or do to take away their pain. And as the reality seemed to settle into her, she couldn't deny that there was some pain within herself. She was suddenly confronted with a very clear memory of Richard Byrnehouse-Davies as he'd taken her hand to walk with her around the house. He'd talked of dying in a way that had made her uneasy, and she wondered now if he'd somehow sensed that it was inevitable. She also wondered if he'd shared his feelings with anyone else. He'd as much as told her not to tell anyone what he'd said, so she doubted he had. Richard was an incredible man, and he'd left an indelible impression on her. But now he'd become a casualty of war. The thought made her tangibly ill. Then she turned to look at the people who loved him most. They had *all* become casualties of war. They, just like every other citizen of the world who had suffered hardship and lost loved ones, had felt the wounds and would be forced to live with the scars. It was tragic and horrible and unfair. And there was nothing to be done about it.

Eight
THE GOOD FIGHT

LeNay gasped when Jesse suddenly came to life. He cursed and kicked the chair he'd been sitting on, then he turned away and walked into the house. Instinctively LeNay followed him, practically running to keep up with his long stride as he hurried down the hall and took the stairs three at a time. She reached his bedroom door just as it slammed in her face. She uttered a silent prayer and tried to feel her instincts. She opened the door and stepped into his room, closing it behind her. He was sitting on the edge of the bed, his back to her.

"I need to be alone," he said, his voice coarse and gruff.

"No," she said, sitting beside him, "you need to be with me."

He seemed tense and frightened, but he said nothing. Knowing him the way she did, it wasn't difficult to guess where his thoughts were.

"Are you afraid to let me see you cry?"

He said nothing, but his eyes agreed.

"Jesse," she took his hand gently, "if you believe we're meant to be together, then you have to believe that the purpose for being together is to carry each other through the struggles of life." She sensed him softening and continued. "I was alone when my mother died. I had no one to lean on or cry with." She looked directly into his eyes and found compassion there. "Please," she swallowed and her voice cracked, "don't leave me alone now. And don't make me leave you alone."

LeNay watched as hot moisture filled his eyes, then he squeezed them shut and tears trickled down his face. He groaned and clutched onto her. She held to him tightly, pressing her lips into his hair, cradling him against her as he wept helplessly. More than an hour passed as he sobbed and heaved, groaned and cursed. And LeNay just held him, crying silent tears on his behalf, holding a prayer in her heart that he would somehow find peace and be able to move on.

His anguish finally calmed into a quiet agony. He curled up like a child on the bed, his face pressed into the folds of her dress while she leaned against the headboard with pillows propped behind her. She pressed her hand repeatedly through his dark hair, tangling its curly waves around her fingers. She didn't even realize she'd been humming until he murmured, "Don't stop."

LeNay took a deep breath and began again, humming the melody of "Amazing Grace." It was a song her mother had often sung or hummed while she'd worked around the house, and it gave LeNay comfort. Something warmed her deeply to realize that it was giving Jesse comfort now. He tightened his hold on her and she bent to kiss his brow. She relaxed against the pillows and continued humming. She felt him gradually soften, and his breathing fell into a calm rhythm. She knew for certain he was sleeping when she stopped humming and he didn't protest.

"I love you, Jesse Hamilton," she murmured to the empty room. "I will be here for you, always."

A short while later, LeNay heard a soft knock at the door. If she got up to answer it, or even called out, she knew Jesse would awaken, only to be confronted again with his grief. She was relieved when the door came open slightly, and Alexa peered inside. Her face showed the evidence that she too had been crying, long and hard. LeNay put a finger to her lips, then motioned with her hand for Alexa to come closer.

Alexa sat carefully on the other side of Jesse, briefly touching his hair as if he were a sleeping baby. LeNay could well imagine Alexa watching over him when he had been. "Is he all right?" Alexa whispered.

LeNay only shook her head. She knew that the peacefulness of his sleeping was only temporary, and the path through his grief would be long and treacherous.

"I worry about him most," Alexa said. "Even more than Richard's parents, really. Jesse practically worshiped Richard." She touched Jesse's hair again. "And he's still so young, so unsure of himself. This is going to be hardest for him." Alexa's eyes focused intently on LeNay, as if to add some silent warning to her verbal one. "Don't let his grief and fears come between you. Don't ever let go of him. Don't ever give up on him. But at the same time, don't allow him to hurt you."

LeNay gazed at Jesse's face, fighting off the uneasiness of such words. *Grief. Fears. Hurt.*

"How are *you?*" LeNay whispered, and fresh moisture brimmed in Alexa's eyes.

"You know," she murmured quietly, "I have missed Jess every hour of every day since I lost him. But I have never . . ." Her voice broke and she squeezed her eyes shut. Her chin quivered and she bit her lip. "I have never needed him so much as I have in the last few hours."

LeNay couldn't hold back her own fragile emotion as she considered Alexa's position. Tyson and Lacey had each other, as did Michael and Emma. Jesse had LeNay. But Alexa had no one. LeNay reached out a hand and took Alexa's, squeezing it tightly. In an effort to console her, she said gently, "Perhaps he is closer than you think."

She was surprised by the warm smile that filled Alexa's countenance, even though the flow of her tears increased. "That's just it, my dear. For the first time since I lost him, I have felt, beyond any doubt, that he was with me."

LeNay's lips parted to draw a deep breath as she grasped what Alexa was saying. While Alexa attempted to compose herself, LeNay felt a warm shiver rush through her, filling her with an inexplicable peace.

"There are no words to explain it," Alexa said. "There was nothing tangible to give what I felt any logical credibility. But . . ." She pressed a fist to her heart and squeezed her eyes closed, as if to hold the memory close. "I know he was there, comforting me. And I could almost hear him telling me that he had taken Richard home, and all was well." She sniffled and wiped a delicate hand over her face to dry the tears. "Somehow I *know* that we will be with him again. We simply must have the faith to move forward and do our best to be happy."

They were both startled when Jesse lifted his head and turned abruptly toward Alexa. He was readily alert, making it evident that he'd been awake long enough to hear what she'd said. "How can you *know*, Grandma?"

Alexa took a deep breath. "I can't explain it, Jesse. I simply believe that—"

"Well, I'm not sure I *can* believe it," he said, shattering the tranquility of the moment as he moved to the edge of the bed and pressed his head into his hands. His voice betrayed anguish as he added, "I don't know how I can go on if he's not coming home."

"You can go on because you have people who love you, people who need you," Alexa said. She gave LeNay a meaningful gaze, then nodded her head discreetly toward Jesse. Taking Alexa's cue, LeNay slipped one hand into Jesse's, relieved to feel him take it firmly. She pressed the other hand over his shoulder.

When nothing was said for several minutes, Alexa said, "The two of you need to eat. You missed supper."

"I can't eat," Jesse said.

"I know it's hard," Alexa said, "but we have to go on." Jesse didn't protest and she added, "I'll bring a tray up."

"I'll go get it," LeNay offered, feeling the need to move around a little. And she sensed that Alexa needed a few minutes alone with Jesse. She returned with a cold supper for the two of them to share, only to find the room empty. It only took a minute to realize that Jesse was not in the bathroom or the sitting room. She hurried to the window and could barely see him walking out across the field in the little remaining light of day.

LeNay hurried down the stairs and outside, fearing he would get in the plane and leave before she could stop him. But she found him standing in his cherished spot in the field, gazing toward the sky. She stopped a short distance from him, saying, "Do you want me to leave you alone?"

He turned abruptly toward her, as if she'd startled him. When he said nothing, didn't even move, she turned to walk away. But she had only taken three steps when he said firmly, "LeNay." She turned back to look at him and found his arm stretched out toward her. She stepped forward and took his hand, relieved to feel him pull her tightly into his arms. "I need you," he murmured.

"I need you too," she said.

Following a long moment of silence, he set his chin on the top of her head and spoke with yearning. "As long as I can remember, Richard was obsessed with flying. He was always making paper airplanes, and studying everything about flight that he could get his hands on. I'll never forget when he talked his father into purchasing a plane, with the justification that it decreased the travel time when we live out in the middle of nowhere. Tyson and my father looked into it and actually invested in a couple of planes, and they covered having some of the hands trained in flying. From that day on, Richard flew everywhere he went. There were a few years that he had some job in town. I don't even remember what it was. I only knew that every morning at seven-twenty he'd be taking off, and every evening he'd come back, somewhere around six o'clock. I would lie out here in the field with my eyes closed, waiting to hear the plane. And after he'd land, he'd always pick me up and turn me around, telling me it was a flying lesson. Every Saturday he'd take me up, unless the weather was really bad. And when I was old enough, he taught me to fly."

Jesse sighed and tightened his arms around LeNay. "I remember feeling jealous when he got married, but he lived here with his wife, and it didn't seem like anything would change. Then his wife died of some serious illness, less than a year after they were married. She was pregnant at the time. It wasn't long afterward that he joined the Air Force. I was devastated. But he reminded me of what he'd told me as a child, that he would always . . ." Emotion choked its way into his voice and he barely managed to say, ". . . That he would . . . find his way home."

"He is home, Jesse. Life goes on." She paused and quoted a familiar thought, "Fight the good fight of faith, lay hold on eternal life."

Jesse drew back to look at her, and she could barely make out his expression in the hovering darkness. Still, it was evident that her words had struck something in him. "Where did you get that?" he asked.

"The Bible," she answered. "First Timothy, chapter six, I believe." When he said nothing more she added, "That's what he did, Jesse. He fought a good fight. And his life hasn't ended. He's just gone on. I believe he's with your grandfather, just like Alexa said. And perhaps he's with his wife. Maybe he's happier now than he's been in a long time. And you have to do what he would want you to do."

"And what is that?" he asked in a curt tone, as if he dared her to actually help him find any peace in this.

"To fight the good fight . . . with faith. To go on living. To go on flying."

Through a sudden sob, Jesse said, "I don't know if I can."

LeNay didn't try to convince him otherwise. She knew it would take time. His pain was raw and all-consuming. He threw his head back and howled his sorrow toward the sky, then he sank to his knees, pressing his face against her belly, his hands to her back. He cried with fresh anguish, and again, LeNay just held him.

Time lost all substance as they ended up lying on the ground, holding each other close, gazing up at the sky. LeNay broke the silence when she pointed toward

Richard's star, saying, "Imagine him there, Jesse." She swept her arm around to create a circle, coming back to the star. "He's flying—flying like he never has before."

She felt him turn to look at her and she moved her gaze to meet his. "I love you, LeNay," he said and urged her closer. Looking down at him, she was barely able to see his expression, but she didn't have any trouble finding his lips as he took her face into his hands and urged her to kiss him. He kissed her and kissed her, as if she could somehow free him of his pain. She found herself looking up at him, his form silhouetted against the night sky.

"I love you, Jesse," she said, and he pressed his face to her shoulder.

A while later, he came to his feet and helped her up. They walked in silence back to the house, where she coaxed him to eat. The following day she found Jesse sticking close to her as the family went through the motions of living. He said practically nothing, reminding her of the days when he'd been trapped in his shyness. Now he was trapped in a shell of grief, but at least he seemed to want LeNay there with him. There was talk of wanting some kind of memorial service, but it was difficult to know what to do when there was no proof of his death. The fact that Richard Byrnehouse-Davies was missing in action came out in all the newspaper headlines, which made some of the family angry. Others seemed indifferent.

Three days after the original telegram arrived, another came reporting that Richard's body had been found. It would be shipped home with full military honors. Even though he'd been presumed dead, the reality seemed to open wounds freshly. The days went by in a blur as they waited for the body to arrive, and then a funeral service was

held. LeNay was amazed at the number of people in attendance, people from all walks of life—even the local farmers,
who seemed as important to the Davies family as the well-
known attorneys and politicians they seemed familiar with.
LeNay couldn't help feeling pride in the countless times she
was introduced as Jesse's fiancée. He kept her continually at
his side, and she felt his need for her. But his quiet, guarded
nature had long ago reached a point of making her feel
somehow left out of his life. She reminded herself that the
process of dealing with grief was different for everyone, and
she needed to allow him the time to come to terms with
Richard's death.

Following the burial, Jesse told her he needed to be
alone. LeNay wandered back out to the little private cemetery, surrounded by a wrought-iron fence, where Richard
had just been laid to rest. LeNay pondered the graves of
Jess Davies and his parents. She thought about the reality
that she, too, would likely be buried here. She turned to
absorb her surroundings and decided she liked the idea of
growing old here, of seeing her children and grandchildren
raised here, just as Alexa had done.

LeNay thought of Richard, and fresh tears came. She
recalled his tenderness toward her, and the sweet kisses
he'd given her. She found it ironic that he had teasingly
called her his cousin. And now, as Jesse's wife, she would
be just that.

LeNay finally went back into the house, still wearing
the slender black dress she'd purchased for the occasion,
carrying her black shoes to ease her aching feet. She felt
restless and habitually wanted to be with Jesse, but he'd
asked to be alone. Instead of searching him out, she
decided to go to the library and seek out a good book.

She caught her breath when she came through the door and found Jesse there. "I'm sorry," she said. "I didn't know you were here. I know you want to be alone, and . . ."

"Come here," he said and she did, only to see that he had a glass of golden liquid in his hand, and a liquor bottle on the little table close by. He swallowed the contents of the glass, then filled it again before he glanced up at her in question. "Well, sit down," he said, his voice slightly slurred.

LeNay sat beside him, feeling hesitant and a little afraid. She could only recall seeing her father drunk on one occasion, and it hadn't been a pleasant experience. She felt disconcerted to realize this man she loved was doing something she didn't know how to confront. She'd never seen him drink before—nothing beyond the usual wine with meals.

"You know," he said, pointing to her shoes with the glass in his hand, "those are the most impractical shoes in the world. But don't throw them away." He took a long swallow and added, "Your legs look great in them. In fact," he leaned his head back on the couch and chuckled, "when you wear those shoes, it makes me feel . . . well, you know."

LeNay glanced down with a timid smile. It seemed the liquor had loosened him up enough to forget his tendency to be guarded.

"But," he said, "I feel that way when you take them off and walk around in those bare feet, too." He lifted one of her feet onto his lap and fondled her ankle. Then he emptied the glass again.

LeNay felt suddenly too uncomfortable to stay under these circumstances. "You're drunk, Jesse," she said, removing her leg from his grasp.

138

"I know," he said with a little laugh. "I haven't felt this good since . . . since . . ." The hardness that came over his face made it clear what he intended to say. Since they'd been informed of Richard's death. But he only said, "I need another drink." LeNay watched him pour more liquor into his glass with unsteady hands. Suddenly feeling the urge to cry, she was ready to turn and leave when she heard the door open behind her.

"LeNay," Alexa said, "have you seen Jesse? I need to—"

"He's right here," LeNay said, stepping aside, wondering if Alexa would know how to handle him.

When Alexa came close enough to get the picture of Jesse drinking himself into oblivion, she flew into what LeNay could only describe as a calm rage. In one agile movement she snatched the glass from Jesse's hand and threw it into the cold fireplace grate, where it shattered. She grabbed the bottle with her other hand and took a long look at the label before she slapped Jesse hard across the face. LeNay winced, then held her breath as Jesse turned scornful eyes toward his grandmother, but Alexa didn't cower even slightly. She pushed her face close to Jesse's and took his chin into her hand.

"Do I have your attention, young man? I would hope so. And I hope you're sober enough to remember this tomorrow, because I will not tolerate this kind of behavior. You have no business bringing hard liquor into my home. We all love him. We all miss him. We're all hurting. But nobody else is trying to drown it in whiskey. It won't change anything. It won't bring him back. It only makes you look like a fool."

Jesse looked briefly humbled, but his expression hardened again as he snarled, "I'd wager you didn't treat Jess Davies like this."

Alexa actually laughed, and for some reason it was easier for LeNay to imagine her being the jockey who won the race that saved this station. "You'd better rethink your bet, Mister Hamilton. One morning Jess Davies woke up with a hangover and no memory of the previous night beyond a good hard slap. Eventually he came to his senses and faced up to his pain instead of trying to drown it in a bottle. That's when he became a man worth marrying. And if you're any kind of a man, you'll be doing the same thing."

"Something wrong?" Michael's voice came from behind LeNay and startled her.

"Your son is drunk," Alexa said. "I'm glad you're here. Don't leave him alone until he's sober. Drunk men have a way of doing stupid things."

Alexa left the room, taking the bottle with her. LeNay could easily imagine her pouring what little was left down the drain. Michael sighed and took hold of Jesse's arm, urging him to his feet. "Come along," he said. "We're putting you to bed."

Jesse cursed under his breath but went along with his father, murmuring to LeNay as he passed by, "Don't forget your shoes."

Nine
FAITH

LeNay went up to her room and had a good cry before she got ready for bed. Alexa came to her room a little after ten. "I wanted to be certain you're all right. I'm sure that wasn't a pleasant experience for you."

"I'm just grateful you came along when you did," LeNay admitted as they sat close together on the edge of her bed. "I wouldn't have known what to do."

"Well, hopefully it will leave an impression. I'm afraid we're just going to have to give him some time to come to terms with this."

"You sound as if you're speaking from experience."

Alexa drew a deep breath. "Far too much experience to get into tonight, love."

"Okay, but . . . I can't help wondering . . . What stupid thing did Jess Davies do when he was drunk?"

"Did I say it was Jess?"

"No," LeNay said, "but . . ."

"You're very perceptive, love. My father did a lot of drinking when I was younger, although he overcame it eventually. But Jess struggled with it when he was confronted with some difficult things in his life. And one night . . . well, one of the stable hands found him trying to mount a horse with a loaded gun in his hand, mumbling about . . . well, it was evident he'd intended to kill himself. Of course, once he sobered up, he was shocked and horrified. I think that was the first step in his coming to terms."

"How did he do it?" LeNay asked.

Alexa sighed. "Some other time. We both need to get some sleep. If Jesse remembers our little conversation in the morning, we could be in for a rough day."

LeNay hardly slept that night. She finally drifted off just before dawn and woke up to the feel of mid-morning. Before she found the motivation to get out of bed, she heard the plane. She rushed to the window, but it was too late. Jesse was nowhere to be seen, and a moment later, even the low hum of the plane engine completely dissipated in the distance. LeNay tried to ward off the deepening dread she felt, but as she turned away from the window, her eyes caught an envelope that had been slid beneath her door. With a trembling hand she picked it up and tore it open to unfold a single page, written in Jesse's hand.

My dearest LeNay, There's something I have to do. I can't expect you to understand. I'm not certain I understand it myself, but it doesn't change the way I feel about you. I don't know how long I'll be, and I pray that one day you will be able to forgive me. You're everything to me. Stay strong, my love, and one day we will be together again.

"One day?" she shouted to her surroundings. Then she finished reading. *I love you with all my heart and soul. Jesse. P.S. Tell Grandma I remember every word.*

LeNay pulled on a robe and hurried down the hall to find Alexa. She read the letter then sighed heavily. "Maybe I was too hard on him."

"Maybe I should have slapped him, too," LeNay retorted. "He loves me with all his heart and soul, except for the part that has to leave and do who knows what for who knows how long."

Alexa sighed again. "You asked me last night about how Jess came to terms with his struggles."

"Yes," LeNay said, not appreciating the change of subject.

"Well, he left home."

LeNay hung her head and sighed, realizing the connection.

"I don't recall exactly how long he was gone, but he came back a different man. We just need to have faith enough to believe that Jesse will do the same."

Three days after Jesse left, LeNay accepted an invitation from Lacey to go into town and do some shopping. She was sick to death of sitting around missing Jesse. But they returned to see the plane parked in the field.

"Oh, good heavens," LeNay murmured and jumped out of the car the moment it came to a halt. She ran into the house and literally bumped into Jesse on the stairs.

"Good, you're here," he said, moving past her. "I didn't want to leave without saying good-bye."

"Leave?" she echoed, following him back outside. "Where are you going?"

"Grandma can explain," he said. His lack of attentiveness made her wonder what had gone wrong between them.

"No!" she shouted, taking hold of his arm to make him stop. "You can explain. And you can do it now. You're the one who told me that forever wasn't long enough for us. And you were going to leave without saying good-bye?"

"I didn't know where you were."

"And you couldn't wait an hour or—"

"I have to go," he said and started walking again.

LeNay ran after him, feeling a desperation unlike anything she'd ever experienced. Something was terribly wrong, and she knew it with every fiber of her being. "Jesse!" she called but he just kept walking with determination toward the plane.

* * * * * * * *

Allison took hold of her grandmother's hand. "Grandma? Are you all right?"

"I'm just . . . so tired," LeNay said feebly.

The nurse appeared at Allison's side. "She really needs to rest. She's been perkier today than she's been in weeks, but it's been a long day for her."

"Of course," Allison said, trying to cover her disappointment, while her mind was screaming: Where was Jesse going? What happened next? How can you expect me to wait?

As if Betsy had read her mind, she smiled at Allison and said, "The story has a happy ending."

"Of course," Allison said. Then to her grandmother, "We'll talk some more later. You rest."

Allison took her tape player and left the room, finding the house eerily quiet. She wandered through the halls, marveling at the thought that this was the very home where LeNay had come to stay with Alexa Davies, the home where Jesse Hamilton was born and raised. The home where his son, Michael, had brought his bride and her three children, including herself. Allison had to rub the chill from her arms as the walls seemed to speak to her of the generations that had been born, lived, married, and died here. She reminded herself that she technically had no blood relation to any of these people. But then, neither did LeNay. Perhaps that was one of many reasons they shared such a deep kinship.

Allison wandered into the library, imagining Jesse Hamilton drunk on the couch, and Alexa throwing the glass into the fireplace. The image became so clear that she almost expected to find broken glass among the ashes. She ambled slowly outside, perusing her surroundings as if she'd never seen them before. Again she felt chilled, as if the memories were her own, rather than something she'd only heard repeated. She walked over to the little cemetery and went inside the wrought-iron gate. Many of the names carved in stone weren't just names to her anymore. Tyson Byrnehouse-Davies, and his wife Lacey. And of course, Richard: 1909 to 1943. There were the graves of Michael and Emma Hamilton, and Jess and Alexa Davies. But Allison didn't really feel emotional until she found the grave of Jesse Michael Hamilton. She squatted beside it and ran her fingers over his name, feeling unreasonably close to him. She thought of the years he'd been gone and felt a new perspective in relation to LeNay's pending death. Was Jesse waiting for her even now, anxious for them to be reunited?

Allison went back into the house when she remembered a stack of photo albums in the lounge room. She'd looked at the pictures many times, but the older ones had meant nothing to her. Until now. She laughed aloud as she opened one with a brown cover and yellowing pages. It only took a minute to realize what it was. She took it and two others up to the room where she was staying.

Since LeNay mostly slept through the evening, Allison spent every minute with the photos except for the time it took to eat a quick supper. She became thoroughly consumed by the hundreds of pictures, laughing at some moments, crying at others. She was amazed at how it felt to actually see these people she'd been hearing about; page after page of black and white pictures: Michael and Emma. Tyson and Lacey. Richard. Alexa, and even Jess Davies before his death. And of course, LeNay and Jesse. There were wedding pictures and snapshots of holidays and birthdays and everyday occurrences. But the pictures that struck Allison the deepest were the ones of Jesse Hamilton with his plane. It was as if someone had taken a camera out to the field and spent the afternoon just snapping pictures. It became evident that the someone was LeNay, when there appeared pictures of her from the same set. Obviously Jesse had taken over the camera. Then someone else must have appeared to do the shooting, since there were pictures of Jesse and LeNay together, with the plane in the background. Allison pulled out a few and set them on her bedside table, then she went to sleep, her thoughts filled with stories that consumed her every nerve. She thought it was a good thing she knew that Jesse and LeNay had ended up together, or she never would have been able to sleep at all. Where was he going? she wondered, and drifted off.

Right after breakfast, Allison found LeNay looking chipper, her eyes sparkling with anticipation. With a fresh tape in the recorder, Allison sat beside the bed.

"Look what I found, Grandma," she said, helping LeNay put on her glasses to look at the pictures Allison had. "This is you and Jesse, isn't it?"

"Oh, it is." LeNay beamed, then she laughed.

"And here. He's really kissing you, I'd say."

"Indeed," LeNay said and visibly blushed. She giggled as if the memories made her tingle.

"But I think I like this one best," Allison said, showing her a photograph of Jesse walking away from the plane. He wore a flight jacket, and his breeches were tucked into high, riding-type boots. His face showed clearly, and his resemblance to his father and grandfather was evident.

"Oh, yes," LeNay said, putting a hand to her heart. "It reminds me of that first day I saw him."

"When you thought he was an arrogant snob."

"Exactly," LeNay said and giggled again.

"But, I have to know, Grandma. Where was he going when you came home from town and found him leaving?"

"Well, that's what I wanted to know," LeNay said. "I was terrified. I couldn't possibly imagine what might be so important to him. And when he told me what he'd done, I wanted to die. I thought I'd never see him again."

* * * * * * * *

"Jesse!" LeNay took hold of his arm again, making him face her. "Don't you walk away from me without an explanation. Talk to me! Now!"

She saw his expression soften before he took her into his arms, holding her with a desperation that matched her own. "I don't expect you to understand why I have to do this. I know it's not fair to you, but . . . it's too late. I have no choice, and—"

"What?" she drew back to look into his eyes. "What do you have to do, Jesse?"

His hesitance combined with his expression was frightening. "I've joined the Air Force," he said without looking at her.

For a long moment she was too much in shock to respond, then a harsh, one-syllable laugh erupted from her throat. "I . . . can't believe it. How could you, when . . ." The full picture began to descend, and an unexplainable fear gripped her every nerve. "No!" she cried, taking hold of him. "We're at war, Jesse."

"You think I don't know that? It wouldn't be long before I'd have to go anyway."

"But . . . the Air Force. Don't you realize the average life expectancy of a fighter pilot in action is six weeks?"

His eyes widened. "Who told you that?"

"Richard told me. He knew how precarious it was, but he didn't want his family to worry. He would *not* want you doing this. Have you gone mad?"

"Perhaps I have," he said, almost sounding regretful.

LeNay suddenly felt so angry she had to turn her back to keep from physically taking this emotion out on him. She clenched her fists and fought the heaving in her chest enough to say, "I've been praying and hoping that you wouldn't be called up before the fighting ended, that you—"

"This war is far from over, LeNay. It's a fact we have to face. I can't sit around any longer just waiting for my number to come up."

"So you *joined?* It's practically suicide!"

"That's what the rest of them said," he countered angrily.

"Because it's true!" She turned back to face him, barely conscious of the tears saturating her face. "What is this? Some attempt to vindicate Richard's death? Is it vengeance? Anger? What, Jesse? Tell me."

"I don't know," he said. "I don't expect you to understand. I just . . ."

"What?" she screamed and took hold of his shoulders. "Help me understand. You told me we were forever. Now you're turning your back on everything we've found together to . . . to . . . What?" she shouted louder. "I don't understand!"

"I don't understand it either, LeNay; not completely, anyway. I only know that a part of me has dreaded bringing this war into our relationship from the first moment I realized that you loved me, too. I have wondered if it was wrong of me to be proposing marriage, to be making promises I'm not in a position to keep."

LeNay was so thoroughly shocked, she couldn't even speak. She pressed her hands to her chest to fight a sudden constriction, much the same way Jesse had done when he'd collapsed on the stairs. With no warning, he took her face into his hands, kissing her as if he might never have the chance again. "I love you," he said, "with all my heart and soul."

"No," she snarled, "there is a very big part of your heart and soul that is so lost in some ridiculous madness that it doesn't know how to love."

He looked as if he'd been slapped. "I have to go," he said and turned to walk briskly toward the plane. LeNay stood where she was, too stunned and hurt to even move. She hated him for doing this to her, for making promises that he wasn't man enough to keep. She wanted to scream at him and tell him to go to hell. But as she watched him getting ready to start the plane, the reality struck her. He was leaving, and she might never see him again.

"Jesse!" she called and ran. She only took a few steps before she had to stop and frantically remove her shoes, tossing them to the ground. She ran toward him, spurred on by a crushing, desperate fear. "Jesse!" she called and he turned toward her, one hand on the propeller. He took two steps toward her before she flung herself into his arms, clinging to him, crying against his throat.

"Please don't leave me," she said. "Please. I need you."

Jesse took hold of her face and looked at her hard. His eyes filled with moisture as he muttered hoarsely, "I have to, LeNay. Maybe it was wrong. Maybe it was stupid. But it's done. It's too late to undo it now. I have to fight the good fight . . . for Richard, for me—and for you. I'm not going to live in fear of being forced to fight for my country. I'm going to do it because I believe in it. Because Richard believed in it."

"Please . . . don't go yet. Surely a day or two won't matter. We need to be together, Jesse. I need some time with you."

Jesse looked into her eyes as if they could make him melt into the ground. His voice was hoarse as he said, "I can't stay, LeNay. Feeling the way I feel, I would do something we'd both end up regretting."

LeNay turned warm as she grasped his implication. He pressed his mouth over hers with a kiss that was brief but harsh. "Pray for me," he whispered as tears spilled down his face. "When I come back we'll get married."

"Marry me now, before you go. Surely we deserve some time to—"

"I can't, LeNay. It would be harder for you. I don't want you to stop living just because I'm gone. If you're married, it would be more difficult. Please try to understand why it has to be this way."

"I don't understand," she said through a surge of fresh tears. "But it's evident that I have to let you go anyway."

Jesse kissed her again then left her standing, helpless and frightened. She watched the plane gain speed and lift into the air, then he circled over her, as low as he possibly could, reaching out a gloved hand toward her as if he could touch her. LeNay lifted her hand in response, turning to follow the plane as it circled once more then disappeared in the distance.

LeNay didn't know how long she stood there, feeling as if the life had been drained from her. She felt helpless to even move back toward the house, and too frozen to even sit down and cry.

"You know," Michael Hamilton's voice startled her and she turned to see him standing close by, his hands behind his back, "I've wondered sometimes if there isn't just something in a man that has to break free before he can settle down and look at life as it really is. Tyson left. I left. Even Jess Davies left. But we all came back eventually, changed and stronger." He chuckled softly. "Maybe it's that walkabout thing. I wonder if only Australian men are like this, or if . . . we just have a word for it."

He paused and LeNay wondered if she was supposed to say something, but her tongue was as frozen as the rest of her. Michael turned his head to look around, as if he'd never seen the view before.

"After raising all those girls, I must confess that Jesse managed to keep me off balance most of the time. And then one day I realized he was a great deal like me." He gave an abrupt laugh. "That's a frightening thought, except that . . . Emma tells me when it came right down to it, my heart was good. And that's what got us through. The good thing about

Jesse is that he has a whole lot of Emma in him. She's sensible. Compassionate. Strong." He paused again and his eyes became intense, making her heart quicken as she sensed something deeper here than an effort to patronize her wounded heart. "It was Emma's love that brought me home, and kept me here."

Tears leaked from LeNay's eyes as she perceived his message. In her heart, she truly believed that the love she shared with Jesse had the power to bring him home. But there were aspects to the situation that could not be controlled by love alone. She steered her thoughts else-where and asked, "Where did you go . . . when you left?"

"Prison, eventually," he said with a smile that made it seem amusing, but eyes that told her it hadn't been.

"I'm glad you came back," she said, thinking as she often did how much she liked this man. Then her eyes went by their own will to the sky above her, as if she could somehow reach Jesse with her thoughts.

"He'll come back," Michael said, as if he'd read her mind.

"How can I be sure?" she asked with fresh emotion. "Richard didn't come back."

Michael sighed and looked up. As he hesitated, she realized that he was fighting emotion. "I'm not very good at answering questions like that," he said. "But I know what Alexa Davies would say." He laughed as if to avoid sobbing. "I can't count the times I've been saved by imag-ining what Alexa Davies would say."

"What would she say?" LeNay asked.

"You tell me."

"I think she'd tell us to have faith and believe."

Michael nodded. "Yeah, that sounds like the great Mrs. Davies." He smiled subtly. "You and I are a special breed,

152

LeNay. We are among the lucky few who get pulled out of the gutter and taken under the wings of Byrnehouse-Davies. But we are even luckier than most, and I know of only one other person who could share what we share. We are the ones lucky enough to actually be loved and made a part of the family."

"I don't believe in luck," LeNay said, and Michael's eyes widened. "I believe that in the long run we get what we work for. Even lucky breaks come to nothing if we throw the chances away. I would bet you're here because you earned it."

"You might have a point there," he said after a minute's silence. "But if that's true, you're here for the same reason. You belong here, LeNay. Whether he comes back or not, you're a part of us." He surprised her by putting his arms around her in a tight, fatherly embrace. She was even more surprised to realize he was crying as he added, "And having you here makes it easier for me to believe that he *will* come back."

He pressed a kiss to her brow then stepped back, wiping his face with his shirtsleeve. "I should get back inside. Emma's very upset."

"That's understandable," LeNay said, and Michael held out a hand toward her. She took it and they walked slowly back to the house, pausing long enough to find her shoes. When she started to cry he put his arm around her, urging her head to his shoulder as they kept walking. She wondered if this was how it would be to have a caring, compassionate father.

"Who else is there?" she asked and he made a noise to indicate he didn't know what she was talking about. "You said there was one other person like us."

"That would be Lacey," he said. "She was found on the street as a child, dressed like a boy. No one ever claimed her, so they raised her along with the twins, then she ended up marrying Tyson."

"Twins?" LeNay asked, and he looked at her in astonishment.

"How long have you been here?" he asked with a laugh that made her realize she felt a little better.

"Apparently not long enough."

"Tyson and Emma are twins."

"Really? I never would have guessed."

Once in the house, Michael left to see to Emma. LeNay could well imagine Jesse's mother curled up on her bed, sobbing helplessly. Feeling an urge to do the same, LeNay went to her room. The tears came quickly when she found Jesse's extra flight jacket on the bed, the one she'd worn when she'd flown with him. And with it was a letter. She wondered how she might have felt to come home after he'd already left and find this here.

Slipping the jacket on, if only to feel closer to him, she sat down and opened the envelope, barely able to read through her continuing tears.

My dear, sweet LeNay, By now you will realize that I'm gone, and you will probably be certain that I'm either stupid or crazy, or maybe both. There's only one thing I can say that matters. I love you, LeNay. You have changed me. I will come home, and we will be together. Forever isn't long enough. Jesse. P.S. The jacket's yours. It was a little small for me anyway. Let it keep you warm while I'm away. But when I come back, we're going to get you some practical shoes. Riding boots, perhaps.

LeNay curled up on the bed and cried herself to sleep, trying to make herself believe that he wouldn't be killed before he had a chance to keep his promises. She dreamed of sitting on the veranda and seeing an official-looking car drive up. The same man got out and walked across the lawn, this time handing the telegram to Michael, who passed it to Tyson, because he couldn't bear to read it himself. She came awake with a start and found Alexa's hand on her face.

"It's time for supper, love," she said. "Come along. You must eat."

LeNay nodded and sat up, orienting herself to the present, then she walked to the dining room with Alexa, pulling the jacket tightly around her.

Days merged into weeks without a word from Jesse. A mood of mourning hovered over the family. It was as if they had just begun to accept Richard's death, when Jesse's absence had slapped them down again. The fact that they were all feeling the same way was evidence of the love and unity they shared.

A letter finally came, directed to the entire family beyond the little note at the bottom which said simply, *I love you, LeNay*. The words he'd written were brief and cryptic. He was fine. He missed them. He hoped all was well at home.

LeNay made a habit of carrying Jesse's jacket with her nearly everywhere she went. As summer settled in fully, it was far too hot to wear it, so she carried it. She hung it over the back of her chair when she ate, and took it with her each day when she'd walk out to the field to Jesse's spot. Sometimes she sat on the jacket. At others she held it to her face and wept, loving the way it still held a subtle aroma of him. It smelled of leather, shaving lotion, and perhaps the sky.

In spite of Jesse's absence, LeNay couldn't deny that her life was good. Unlike in the past, she felt her place with these people, rather than wandering idly about with no particular purpose. She was Jesse Hamilton's fiancée, and the family had made it repeatedly clear that whether he ever came back to marry her or not, she was as good as family to them. This, among other things, couldn't help but make her feel especially blessed—or, as Michael Hamilton would say, *among the lucky few.*

LeNay found that her days were much as they'd been before she'd fallen in love with Jesse. She helped with a little bit of everything, feeling a sense of pride as her love for Jesse made every aspect of the station and the family businesses mean something far deeper than simply a job. As she involved herself with work in the stables, the garden, the house, even the boys' home, she realized that Alexa, Lacey, and Emma did much the same thing. She couldn't help wondering if Alexa had purposely assigned her to work in such a way because she had hopes that LeNay would eventually become a part of the family, and she'd wanted her to become familiar with all aspects of their world. Alexa had admitted that she'd wondered if LeNay might be right for Jesse. She marveled at Alexa's insight, and she tried to have Alexa's faith that everything would turn out all right.

LeNay was actually dismayed to realize that December had arrived and Christmas was approaching. But it quickly became evident that she wasn't the only one who felt that way. LeNay had trouble thinking of celebrating the holiday with Jesse absent, and his parents admitted to feeling the same way. Tyson and Lacey were still struggling deeply with Richard's loss.

Ten days into the month, Alexa stood up from the breakfast table, saying firmly, "I've had about enough of this nonsense from all of you. It's past time to start preparing for Christmas, and we will remember why we celebrate this holiday. We must have the faith to go on in spite of Richard's absence, and the faith to believe that Jesse will come home. We have much to be grateful for. Foremost, we have each other. And I will not tolerate any more of this moping about as if the world had ended. Life is going on, and we will make the most of it—together."

She announced at lunch that the women would be going into town the following day to begin their Christmas shopping. LeNay didn't really want to go, but she didn't want Alexa to be disappointed in her, so she did her best to behave cheerfully. Driving into town with Emma at the wheel, LeNay couldn't help recalling the day she'd come here. Then a thought occurred to her. "You know," she said, "it was exactly one year ago today that you ladies found me and brought me home."

"Really?" Emma said with a little laugh. "It seems like you've been with us forever."

"How did you remember the date so exactly?" Lacey asked.

"Because I left home the day after my birthday, and I was on the bus for two days, and . . ." She stopped when she realized that all three women were glaring at her. Emma was the first to look away, since she was driving. "What?" she asked.

"We missed your birthday?" Lacey said, as if she was terribly appalled.

"Good heavens, girl," Alexa said. "We won't be having any such secrets from now on." Then she laughed. "It would seem we'll be making a slight adjustment in our plans today."

"It would seem so," Emma said.

"Not only that," Lacey added, "since it's LeNay's anniversary of coming to live with us, I think we should go out for a really fine lunch."

"Excellent idea," Alexa said.

They *did* enjoy a fine lunch and filled the trunk with Christmas gifts through the course of the day. But they also insisted on having LeNay pick out something special for herself. They finally settled on buying her a new dress. It was dark green and elegant, the finest thing she'd ever worn. "Maybe you could wear it for Christmas," Emma said when they were coming out of the dress shop.

"Maybe," LeNay said, not wanting to admit aloud that she had no desire to wear it until Jesse came home.

"Maybe we should get her some new shoes to go with it," Lacey suggested.

"My shoes are fine," she said, wondering whether to laugh or cry at her memory of Jesse's related comments.

"How about some riding boots?" Emma asked.

"No," she said so vehemently that all eyes turned to her as if to question her defensiveness. In a softer voice she explained, "Jesse told me he'd buy me some when . . . he comes home."

Alexa squeezed her hand and LeNay added, "Thank you for the dress. You're really too good to me."

"Nonsense," Alexa said, and they drove toward home.

After supper, LeNay walked out to Jesse's spot in the field and sat down. She thought how very blessed her life was in spite of Jesse's absence. There was only one problem—Jesse's absence just made the rest of her life feel so empty. She found it ironic: now that she had come to feel as if she belonged here and had a place, Jesse was gone and she wondered if she could bear staying here without him much longer. When it came right down to it, she felt certain she really didn't belong here without him.

She was surprised when Alexa walked out and sat down beside her. LeNay couldn't recall ever seeing her out here before.

"It's been a while since we've talked," the older woman said.

"What is there to talk about?"

"We could talk about what it will be like when Jesse comes home."

"I can't even imagine."

"Of course you can," Alexa said. "When you feel the lowest, the best thing you can do is close your eyes and remember. Think of how it felt to ride with him, fly with him, hold him in your arms. That's what I do when I miss Jess, and it truly keeps me going. It makes me believe that somehow, in another time and place, we will be together again."

"You're an inspiration to me, Alexa," she said. "I am truly blessed to be here. I could never describe what you've done for me, all you've taught me. But . . ."

"But?" Alexa pressed when she hesitated.

"I don't know if I can stay. With Jesse gone, it just doesn't feel right."

"Would you have us all missing you as well?" Alexa asked.

LeNay swallowed hard. "I don't want to hurt anyone, but . . . I think I might need to go somewhere else . . . for a while at least. Nothing seems right without Jesse."

"And no matter where you go, it won't feel any differently."

LeNay couldn't argue with that, but she had a point to make. "Still, being here . . . the memories are everywhere I turn."

"I understand. You have to do what you feel is best. But when he comes back, he'll come here. And he'll want you."

"I'll keep in touch, of course," LeNay said. "You'll always be able to find me."

Alexa nodded, seeming emotional. "You must stay through the holidays, at least," she insisted.

LeNay wanted to tell her that the holidays would be more difficult than any other time of year. But she had to think of Alexa, and Jesse's parents. Leaving before Christmas would be selfish and insensitive, and she knew it. "Of course," she said and looked toward the sky.

"There's something I want you to have," Alexa said and held out her hand.

LeNay gasped to see the diamond pendant and gold chain that she had worn the night Jesse had confessed his love to her. "Oh, I couldn't possibly," she said.

"I won't miss it," Alexa insisted, fastening the clasp around LeNay's throat without her permission. "And I think you need it more than I do. But I want you to know what Jess told me when he gave it to me. We'd had many years together, and at the time it was difficult to imagine the tremendous struggles we'd endured in times past. But he told me the tear-shaped diamond made him think that sometimes we just have to experience some pain in order to bring positive things into our lives, and to appreciate all that's good."

Alexa embraced LeNay tightly, then she drew back and smiled. "And remember," she said. "Remember the good times, and keep that faith in your heart strong. Faith gives us the ability to keep going no matter what happens."

Ten
THE GIFT

LeNay did her best to follow Alexa's admonition to enjoy the advent of Christmas in spite of how deeply she was hurting. She managed to keep up a good front when she was around the family, staying actively involved in all the preparations. But in solitude, LeNay couldn't hold back the hovering ache of Jesse's absence, and the fear that she might never see him again. She often thought of him saying that they would be married before Christmas. If not for Richard's death, they would have been. She cursed the war for taking his life, and for taking Jesse away from her. She thought of the thousands of women all over the world, lonely and aching as she was now. Mothers and grandmothers. Sisters and aunts. Wives and fiancées. All waiting and wondering, trying to go on with life, never knowing if tomorrow might be the day that would bring the dreaded telegram. She recalled what Richard had said about the broken hearts caused by the war, and she found his insight chilling somehow.

LeNay continually reminded herself to have faith, as Alexa had suggested. But she also had to remind herself of words she'd once spoken to Richard after he had asked her about destiny in relation to young men being shipped across the sea and shot down for the sake of freedom. *If they make it home, then they're meant to make it home,* she'd said. If she truly believed that, then no amount of faith on her part would bring Jesse back if it wasn't meant to be. But the thought of him never coming home was so painful that she couldn't even entertain it. She forced such thoughts away, not willing to admit that he might not come back alive. If that was faith, then she would fight with everything inside of her to feel it.

Less than a week before Christmas, LeNay found that her efforts to keep up this facade of enjoying herself were wearing thin. But it became evident she wasn't the only one pretending when she happened to step into the doorway of the lounge room soon after supper, without being noticed. Emma was crying to her mother. LeNay stepped into the hallway and leaned against the wall, squeezing her eyes shut tightly as she listened to Emma express her fears that were so much like LeNay's. She couldn't keep from imagining his plane going down, his body never being found. LeNay left then, hurrying up to her room to be alone before the hurricane of emotion burst out of her. She curled up on her bed and cried, much the way Jesse had soon after word had come of Richard's plane going down.

LeNay finally drifted off to sleep, physically drained and emotionally numb. She woke up somewhere in the middle of the night with one blatant thought staring at her through the darkness. What if he didn't come back? Could she even go on? She recalled Jesse asking that very question after he'd lost Richard. The loss had driven him to a course of action that made little sense and left behind a trail of pain. Would she end up doing something equivalent? Would the remainder of her life be lost and wasted? If she couldn't comprehend even living without Jesse, how could she *possibly* go on?

The intensity struck her so deeply that she rushed down the hall to Alexa's room, not caring about the time. She knocked and went in without waiting for a response, groping her way to the bedside table from the glimmer of the hall light.

"Alexa," she cried, turning the switch on the lamp. "Alexa, I need to talk to you."

"What is it, love?" Alexa asked, quickly becoming coherent. She sat up and leaned against the headboard, taking LeNay's hand into hers as she sat on the edge of the bed.

"What if he doesn't come back?" she asked with so much emotion that she wondered if Alexa could even understand her. "What if I don't have enough faith? What if he doesn't come home? How can I go on? How can I—"

Alexa leaned forward and took LeNay's shoulders into her delicate hands. "And what if he doesn't?" she countered firmly, almost shaking LeNay. "Faith is not some extraordinary equation that brings about our desires. Don't be thinking that if you come up with enough of it, it will serve as a magic potion to bring him back. Faith is accepting God's will, whatever it may be. It's finding peace in your heart no matter what life may dish out to you. That's why we celebrate Christmas, love. We are Christians. And that means we can go on through this vale of sorrow because the Lord Jesus suffered for us, he died for us, he lives for us. And through him we can find peace and go on."

"But . . . how can I if—"

"Because you're stronger than you think you are," Alexa insisted. "Yes, it hurts. It hurts more than anything to lose someone you love, but in my heart I believe that we prove ourselves worthy of being with those we love again by persevering with faith in spite of their loss. I've lost many loved ones to death. But there are silver linings in every cloud, love. Michael and Tyson both fought in World War I. They came home and raised beautiful families. My life is rich and full, and I am very blessed. And I will not stop living it just because I've had to experience loss and pain. It's a part of life, LeNay. There is no way around it."

Alexa relaxed and her voice softened as she pulled LeNay to her shoulder, holding her like she would a frightened child. "My heart aches for you," she murmured while LeNay cried helplessly. "We will pray for his safe return, and we will make the most of what he left behind."

LeNay cried long and hard, but Alexa just held her, soothing her with gentle words and a loving touch. LeNay thought back to the day Alexa had found her huddled on the street, and the continual love she'd received from this great woman ever since. And now, Alexa's comfort meant more to LeNay than she could ever put into words.

It wasn't until a few days later that the reality of all that Alexa had said began to settle in. Her words had given LeNay encouragement, and she had determined to face her life with courage and make the most of Christmas in spite of the circumstances. But her emptiness had not gone away, and a part of her felt bitter and angry. Then something began to change.

LeNay first felt it when she saw Tyson and Michael coming into the yard with the Christmas trees they had just brought down from the mountains. In a single instant she could almost see the many Christmases gone by when the same ritual had taken place, and the countless Christmases to come when it would continue to happen. She suddenly felt as if she was watching the custom through a haze. Sounds seemed distant, images vague and dreamlike. The year she had been here seemed suddenly like eternity, as if no life had existed before it, and no life would continue beyond this moment.

That timeless, weightless sensation hovered with LeNay through the following days. As she willed herself to participate in the necessities of preparing for Christmas, she felt as if everything going on around her was somehow dreamlike and distant. She felt detached from her surroundings, as if she were some kind of student in the laboratory of life, expected to learn something very important, but completely ignorant on the theory being presented. LeNay expected the feeling to relent, but as the girls began arriving with their families, it only deepened. She was assaulted by a mixture of emotions as Jesse's sisters and cousins expressed their joy in having her a part of the family, and at the same time their concern for Jesse.

The evening before Christmas Eve, everyone gathered in the lounge room, just as they had done the year before. They were talking, laughing, and listening to Christmas music. Then someone made the comment that it had been about this time last year that Richard had appeared. The room became eerily silent. Even the children seemed to sense the gravity of the moment. Then the tears began to flow. The entire mood shifted as the family shared expressions of their ongoing grief, of their disbelief that Richard was really gone.

Then talk shifted to Jesse, and LeNay was grateful for the continuing sensation of being distanced from everything around her, which made it possible for her to sit and listen to what was being said without falling apart. She wiped a few stray tears and absorbed the compassionate glances directed toward her. But then, a marvelous thing happened. The conversation gradually shifted back to where it had begun, and they were all soon laughing and reminiscing once again. A part of LeNay felt a little disconcerted to think that a person could be removed from those who loved him most, and life could go on so easily. No, she corrected, not easily. But something bigger and deeper within herself felt an indescribable kind of peace to see the tangible evidence around her that life *did* go on.

LeNay slept better that night than she had since Jesse had left. And she wondered why. She awoke just before dawn, feeling an urge to be in the room where the entire family had been sitting the previous evening. Impulsively she lit a candle that sat in her room more as decor than anything. But she almost feared the brightness of electric light, thinking it might somehow disperse the dreamlike sensation surrounding her.

LeNay moved carefully down the stairs, intrigued by the shadows cast by the candle's flame that guided her through the darkness. The lounge room felt eerily silent and empty in contrast to its having been filled beyond its capacity the previous evening. LeNay held the candle high and took in the Christmas tree, covered with hundreds of little decorations, many that had symbolic or sentimental significance. Then her eye was drawn to a small nativity scene crafted out of wood. She had noticed it many times and admired its simple beauty. But only now did it seem to hold some spell over her—as if the answers to her deepest questions lay there in the tiny manger.

LeNay felt no drastic or miraculous change occur inside of her as she might have hoped. But as she sat on the floor, gazing at the little figures of the nativity, one by one, she felt a glimmer of something warm and peaceful. She didn't understand it. But she did feel a little better.

LeNay became so lost in her thoughts that she was startled to realize the room had become light, and she could hear evidence of the household coming awake. Realizing she was in her nightgown, she peeked into the hallway and hurried up the stairs, grateful to make it to her room unseen.

Through the day, LeNay still felt as if her surroundings were distant and hazy somehow. But instead of feeling cloaked with bitterness and pain, she felt a layer of something peaceful cloaking her raw emotions. As the activities of Christmas Eve unfolded, she found herself caught up in them, marveling at all that was good in her surroundings and circumstances. It was difficult to believe she'd only experienced all of this once before. It all felt so comfortable that she could almost believe she'd been here forever—or perhaps she was meant to be here at least that long. Jesse's absence, as always, made such thoughts dubious at best. She recalled hearing someone say last year that Jesse had never missed the Christmas Eve traditions. The thought made her ache inside. But even in his absence, the memory of how he loved her and what he meant to her somehow made everything going on around her mean more.

Getting dressed for the excursion to the boys' home, LeNay ached to wear the green dress she'd been given for her birthday. But she reminded herself that she would wear it for Jesse when he came home, and wore instead the pink dress Alexa had given her. The memories associated with it were poignant under the circumstances, but wearing it made her feel somehow closer to Jesse. She put on her black shoes, wishing she could wear them without remembering Jesse Hamilton unfastening their straps and carrying them for her. Impulsively she picked up the flight jacket he'd given her and carried it.

As they set out toward the boys' home with the children in the wagon, LeNay felt emotion hovering in her throat. She hardly dared speak for fear of betraying it. She couldn't decide if she wanted to cry because she desperately missed Jesse, or if she was finally coming to believe that she could go on no matter what course her life took. Either way, she had to fight to keep her tears from erupting.

When Murphy appeared as Father Christmas, passing out gifts to the boys, it occurred to LeNay that she would like to spend more time here, helping with these children. She wondered if Michael might be willing to give her a more permanent job with some specific purpose, and she decided to talk to him about it at the first opportunity. As the idea settled in, she thought how such a thing might help her feel at home here, even in Jesse's absence.

LeNay tuned back to the Christmas celebrations going on around her. The fact that she had participated in all of this a year ago somehow added to the hazy, dreamlike sensations surrounding her. She thought of how Jesse had been here last year, and how she had thought him arrogant and not worthy of a second glance. She recalled his confessions of being drawn to her even then, and a surge of happiness invaded her sorrow. Nothing seemed right without him, and yet, in a way, having loved him made everything seem right. And then she understood.

Instantly the haze filtered away, and she was suddenly seeing her surroundings up close and with reality. The noises of laughter and celebration were louder and more defined. The answer was not in the little manger alone. That was only the beginning. The answer was all around her. It was in being the recipient of so much love and abundance. And in being given the opportunity to give and love in return. The answer was in the basic goodness of life, the simple pleasures and joy that could be found even among the horrors of war and death. The answer was in the children's faces, radiating hope for a bright tomorrow, and for their instinctive belief that they were part of something blessed and wonderful. Not unlike LeNay.

Before they left the boys' home for the walk back to the house beside the wagon, LeNay knew in her heart that she *could* go on without Jesse. She would hurt, yes. If he never came back, she would mourn his loss deeply, and a part of her would never let go of the love she felt for him, or the heartache of his absence in her life. But then, she couldn't deny that she was a better woman for having loved him, and even for having been without him. She had learned something she hadn't expected, something that suddenly made Alexa's words ring in her ears with perfect clarity and understanding. *Faith is accepting God's will, whatever it may be. It's finding peace in your heart no matter what life may dish out to you. That's why we celebrate Christmas . . . And that means we can go on through this vale of sorrow because the Lord Jesus suffered for us, he died for us, he lives for us. And through him we can find peace and go on.*

In an instant, everything changed. And yet, it hadn't happened in an instant. What she felt now was the result of days and weeks of prayer and searching. And as thoughts came together like the pieces of an intricate puzzle, LeNay felt as if she could see the world through new eyes. The sorrow was still there. The ache for Jesse had not gone away. But deep inside, LeNay felt peace. She thought of all those throughout the world affected by this war and felt hope, even for them. She knew beyond any doubt that Christ *did* live. And because of him, even the deepest suffering would be atoned for. And *that*, LeNay knew, was the true meaning of Christmas.

After their return to the house, the children were ushered inside, and LeNay impulsively walked the other direction. The sky was overcast and she actually appreciated the slightly chilly breeze in the air, which allowed her to wear the flight jacket without being uncomfortably warm. And she carried her shoes. As she ambled slowly over the well-used path toward Jesse's cherished spot in the field, the setting sun lit up the clouds over the horizon in brilliant hues of pink and orange.

LeNay stood in the familiar spot for several minutes, contemplating the beauty of the sunset. She counted her blessings one by one, reminding herself of all that was good. But when it came to Jesse's absence, she couldn't help feeling the ache in spite of the peace and understanding she had come to. She wondered how Alexa had been able to live without her beloved Jess so courageously, after they'd shared so much of their lives together. The answer was evident. One day at a time, with courage and faith.

LeNay didn't want to cry, but the tears came with force and she sat down in the tall grass, tucking her legs up beneath her skirt, crying so hard that it hurt her chest and head. When the emotion became too much to bear, she reminded herself of Alexa's admonition. *When you feel the lowest, the best thing you can do is close your eyes and remember. Think of how it felt to ride with him, fly with him, hold him in your arms.*

LeNay lifted her face skyward, closing her eyes tightly. She willed the memories closer and felt a smile come to her face. She could almost feel his kiss against her lips. She could smell the mountain air and feel the saddle beneath her, with Jesse's arms around her as they rode. She could feel the thrill of flying with him. A little laugh erupted from her lips as she recalled how he would tip the wings to make her scream, and then he'd laugh. She heard his laughter fill the air around her, and the hum of the plane engine rang in her ears. She turned her mind to the memory of lying in the field with him, sleeping beneath the starlit sky. Her memories were still and quiet, just as that night had been. But the hum of the plane was still there.

LeNay opened her eyes, startling herself out of the memories. The colors in the sky had lessened. The sun was almost out of sight. But she wondered if she was losing her mind as the hum of a plane filled the air around her, becoming steadily louder. She looked up frantically, her heart pounding. But the sky was overcast with low, thin clouds, and she couldn't see anything beyond them. The roar of the plane became so loud that it drowned out her audible sobbing as she feared there might be some other explanation for the sound she was hearing. With her shoes in one hand she turned frantically, crying toward the sky with all the strength her lungs could muster, "Jesse! I'm here! Oh, Jesse!"

As if in direct response to her words, the tip of a wing emerged through the clouds, then in a heartbeat the plane appeared like some kind of phantom emanating from the mist. It only took another heartbeat for LeNay to know beyond any doubt that it was him. She cried harder than she had when he'd left as she watched him circle over her. With her arm stretched out toward him, she followed the sweep of the plane. He reached out a hand in response, as if he could touch her.

Her sobbing turned to laughter as the plane swept away to a place where he could turn and make a safe landing. It rolled toward her, slowing, then coming to a stop. She was vacillating between laughter and sobbing when the engine became still, leaving her cries all too audible in contrast to the silence. His anticipation was evident in the way he jumped out of the plane and tossed the goggles into the seat. He took a few steps toward her, then hesitated, as if he was wondering how to approach her. She moved toward him only a step before he broke into a run, as if that was all the incentive he needed. They came together with such force that he had to turn with her in his arms or defy the laws of motion.

"Oh, you are real," he murmured into her hair, crushing her against him with her feet dangling above the ground. He kissed her hard then pressed his lips to her throat, murmuring over and over that he loved her, he'd missed her, he needed her. LeNay threw her head back and laughed with pure joy. Jesse responded by turning until they were both dizzy.

"Put me down," she insisted when he teetered and laughed, attempting to gain his equilibrium.

"Not a chance," he said, his face close to hers. A look of mischief came into his eyes just before he pressed his hands to her back and twirled again, giving her no choice but to wrap her legs around his waist. Leaning back against his hands, with her arms outstretched, a shoe in each hand, she truly felt as if she was flying.

Jesse laughed again. "There now," he said, "we've had a proper greeting. But I'm still not going to put you down."

"I'm not complaining," she said, wrapping her arms around his neck. He carried her toward the house as if she weighed nothing. "Oh, Jesse, I can't believe it. You're really here."

"I really am. And I'm staying."

She looked into his eyes. "But how can you, when . . ."

"Shhh," he said and kissed her quickly. "I'll tell you later."

As they approached the house, LeNay wondered why no one had come out to meet him. Surely they would have heard the plane. Jesse set her down just inside the door, giving her a long, savoring kiss. "Oh," he sighed deeply and urged her closer, "I've missed you so desperately."

"Yes, I know what you mean," she said and kissed him again. She laughed aloud. "I can't believe it. You're really here. I think you'd better say hello to your family."

"Good idea," he said. "We can kiss later."

"I'm counting on it," LeNay said and took his hand, leading him up the long hall toward the front of the house. As they approached the parlor, it became evident that Christmas music was playing on the phonograph, which explained why no one had heard the plane. LeNay peered into the room first, noting it was just Alexa, Michael, and Emma. "Where is everybody?" she asked.

"Oh, they just barely went upstairs," Alexa said. "Is something wrong?"

"No, I just . . . have a Christmas surprise for you. I was just given the most wonderful gift of my life, but if you're nice to me, I'll share it with you."

She laughed as Jesse stepped into the doorway and his parents and grandmother all gasped in unison. Emma was the first to come to her feet, hugging Jesse tightly and crying with relief. Then Alexa took her turn. And then Michael. Everyone was crying. Even Jesse.

"I expected you to come home in uniform," Emma said, and Jesse's eyes darted away with obvious tension.

"Maybe you'd better sit down." He looked at LeNay. "All of you."

LeNay's heart quickened. He was home, and he'd said he was staying. But what did that mean? If he'd joined the Air Force, he wouldn't be staying unless something was wrong. Had he left illegally? Would there be trouble ahead?

Jesse was the only one who remained standing. "Well, there's good news and bad news." He sighed and glanced around the room at the people who loved him most. "The bad news is . . . I have a defective heart."

When he offered nothing more, Emma said, "What does that mean? I don't understand."

"There's something wrong with my heart, Mother. I've been told what I can do to keep it under control as much as possible. But the fact is, my heart will probably keep me from living a long life."

He looked directly at LeNay, then he glanced away and went on. "The good news is that . . . well, because I have a defective heart, the Air Force didn't want me. I look at it this way: it may take my life in the long run, but it likely saved my life now. I guess you could say that it saved me from my own stupidity. So . . . here I am. And with any luck, I'll be . . ."

They were interrupted as Tyson, Lacey, and two of their daughters came into the room. "It is you!" Tyson said, crossing the room to embrace Jesse firmly. "The children said they'd heard a plane, but I thought it was their imagination."

Jesse laughed and hugged Lacey and the girls. A few minutes later his sisters appeared, and he had to tell the story again. It was over an hour later before Jesse and LeNay could slip away to be alone. He took her hand and led her outside. Once beyond the house, he turned with no warning and took her into his arms, kissing her as if there was no life for them beyond this moment.

"Oh, LeNay," he murmured, "how I prayed you would still be here. Can you ever forgive me for being such a fool?"

"You're here now. That's all that matters. I'm just so grateful that you're safe, that you don't have to go again."

He embraced her again then took her hand, leading her across the field. "We have to talk," he said.

"I'm listening," she told him when he didn't go on.

But nothing more was said until he had determined the correct spot in the field and sat there, pulling her into his lap.

"So talk," she said.

Jesse sighed and held her tightly. "I have a bad heart, LeNay."

"So you said."

"Can you commit your life to a man, knowing that his life may be brief?"

"I will take every minute we have together and live it to its fullest," she said. "But you must promise you'll be careful, and take good care of yourself."

"I promise," he murmured. Then his voice cracked. "I don't want to die, LeNay. I realized it somewhere in the air after I'd joined the Force and I was coming home to say good-bye. I don't know what kind of madness got hold of me. I'm only grateful that I've been given the chance to live, to share the rest of my life with you."

"I'm grateful too, Jesse." A moment later she said, "I get the feeling you're upset about something. I'm not going to coax it out of you."

He sighed. "Which do you think is worse? Taking a plane up into the sky with the knowledge you could be shot down and killed, or finding out there's something wrong that could kill you without any warning?"

"That's easy for me to answer, Jesse. But what do *you* think?"

"I cried most of the way home. I was so relieved to be expelled that it took a while for the reality to hit me. And when it did, I was terrified. I started praying. I told God that I wanted a chance to live my life with you. I wanted us to have children and see them grow up. I can't tell you how or why, but suddenly something changed in me. If I didn't know better, I could swear that Richard was there, telling me to go home."

"Maybe he was," LeNay said, and Jesse's countenance softened.

"Maybe he was," he repeated. "All I know for certain is that I couldn't get home fast enough. I knew somehow that Richard was where he needed to be, and that I needed to be with you for as long as God will allow. And that's when I began imagining taking you in my arms to give you a flying lesson, just the way Richard did with me. And I figured if I could do that and not fall over dead, my heart was probably strong enough to make it through some good years with you."

He laughed softly and tightened his arms around her. "But then," he said earnestly, "the cloud cover got me all confused. I knew I was close, but I was afraid to come through, not certain if I'd hit the field or the stable. I started praying again, and I could see you so clearly in my mind, like a star to guide me home, waiting there in the field. I could have sworn I heard you call my name, but that's impossible, isn't it? With the noise from the engine, I just didn't think it was possible. But I took a deep breath and came through, and there you were, just the way I remembered you." He chuckled and nuzzled his face into her hair. "Standing there in that dress, with your shoes in your hand."

"I *did* call your name," she said, wondering if there had been a little divine intervention amplifying the sound of her voice. Whatever happened, she was just glad to have him here now.

"I know," he murmured. "And since I survived the flying lesson, there's something I need to ask you." He took her hand into his.

"Okay," LeNay said, and gasped to feel something slide onto her finger.

"Will you marry me?" he asked.

LeNay laughed and held the ring close to her face, barely able to make out what it looked like in the light of a partial moon. She looked into Jesse's eyes and knew that whatever life they shared together would be worth anything she had to face once he left her. But in spite of how difficult she knew that would be, she knew she would get by, just as Alexa had managed without Jess. She thought of Alexa's belief that she would be with Jess again, and she knew that whatever life brought to her, she would follow the example of this great woman. She would have the faith to believe that she and Jesse could be together forever, no matter how brief their time together on this earth might be.

"I love you, Jesse Michael Hamilton," she said.

"I love you, too," he replied. "But that doesn't answer my question."

"Of course I'll marry you," she said, and then he kissed her.

* * * * * * * *

"I've often thought," LeNay said to Allison, "that the star guiding him home on Christmas Eve was somehow like the star that led the shepherds and wise men to the stable where Christ was born. To me it was a miracle. I'd never been so happy in my life." LeNay gazed at the decades-old photograph of Jesse Hamilton that she held in her aged fingers. "Of course, I wore the green dress on Christmas Day, and a few days later he took me into town to buy me some new shoes. They were black and very elegant, but they were easier on my feet."

"And did he get you riding boots?" Allison asked.

"He did. He said it was a reward for learning to ride so well. I told him I had a good teacher." She laughed softly and went on. "We were married just a few weeks after Christmas. I wore Alexa's wedding gown, and we exchanged our vows in the upstairs hall of this house, the very place where all the others had been married. And that's where Michael married your mother."

"I remember it well," Allison said. When LeNay seemed distracted, she attempted to steer the conversation back. "So, I'm assuming the gift you received that Christmas was having Jesse return safely."

"Yes, that was wonderful. But it's not the most important thing I received. It was the faith. Alexa taught me the true meaning of faith that year, in a way that I don't believe I would have been able to learn if Jesse hadn't left. When I looked at it that way, I was almost grateful that he had gone away, but even more grateful that he came home safely to me; to all who loved him.

"That Christmas was a memorable one," LeNay said with a tender smile. "And I'll forever be grateful for the faith. It was what got me through another Christmas that stands out in my memory, mostly because it started out to be one of the most difficult."

"More difficult than having Jesse gone, and not knowing if he'd come back?"

"In a way, yes," LeNay said. "But I think we'd better save that for this afternoon. I am feeling a little tired, and I think it's nearly lunchtime."

"Of course," Allison said and discreetly turned off the recorder. She thought of all she'd managed to get on tape and had the urge to give Ammon a great big hug. He would never know what it meant to her to have this time with her grandmother. He would never know the wonderful gift he'd given her in making this possible. And she would forever be grateful.

Eleven
LOSSES

Later that day when Allison returned to resume their visit, LeNay began in a way that made it evident she had been thinking of the things they'd talked about.

"You know," she said, "looking back, I believe the love Jesse and I shared was so wonderful that it was easier to live without him than I thought it would be. That might sound funny, but he gave me so much that was good. It was as if he had poured so much happiness into me that it has over-flowed through these years without him. Not that it's been easy, but . . ." Her eyes got a familiar dreamy look. "But still, I wouldn't trade the years we had together for anything."

"It's been a long time," Allison said, fighting back the temptation to cry.

"Yes, it has," LeNay said distantly. "It was Jesse's heart that killed him in the end," she added with a distinct sadness in her eyes.

"I thought he died of cancer," Allison said, recalling what her father had told her years ago.

"No," LeNay said. "He got cancer when Michael was about eight, I believe. But it wasn't the cancer that killed him. He responded well to the treatments. But his heart wasn't strong to begin with. He was just never the same after that. Those years were filled with illness for him. He finally died of heart failure when Michael was eleven."

Sensing that LeNay was being drawn too much into sadness, Allison changed the subject. "So, tell me about the Christmas that was more difficult than having Jesse gone."

"Oh my," LeNay said, closing her eyes as if to see the memories. But Allison had become accustomed to the way she kept her eyes closed much of the time as she spoke. "Well, it would have been about four years after Jesse and I were married. Katherine was three at the time." She gave a soft laugh. "Oh, Jesse loved that child. I often wondered if any man had ever been happier to be a father. She was with him a great deal, hanging on his back or walking with her hand in his. And Katherine brought so much happiness to Alexa. Her health deteriorated through those years, but Katherine would sit beside her and look at picture books endlessly. She was always drawing pictures for Alexa, and making her laugh.

"Of course, the war was over by then. Some things were still difficult to come by, but we had everything we needed. I worked in the boys' home some with Jesse, and I even helped with the horses. I spent a lot of time with Emma and Lacey, and it became evident that with time I would take over the running of the household, which they had been doing together for many years. Life was good for us. And then we lost Alexa . . . very suddenly. One morning she just didn't wake up."

Allison unconsciously pressed a hand to her heart. Through LeNay's stories, Alexa had come so much to life. She actually felt a tangible heartache at the thought of her death. Feeling deep compassion, she leaned closer to LeNay, anxiously waiting to hear what she might say.

"Of course her loss was difficult for all of us. Soon afterward, I got pregnant again, and we were thrilled, especially since it had taken time for some reason. The baby was due just a week or so before Christmas. Jesse talked about having a son to carry on his name, since he was the last Hamilton in his line. But then, I lost the baby."

"Oh, no," Allison said. "That must have been horrible."

"It was very difficult, yes," LeNay said. "I had been far enough along that they could tell it was a boy. Jesse was very sweet and encouraging, but I knew the loss hurt him deeply as well.

"I've always loved Christmas, you know," LeNay said, "especially after I came to live here. But that particular year, when I realized that Christmas was coming, I felt sick with dread. It was our first Christmas without Alexa, and it just didn't seem right to be celebrating without her. And how could I help but think that I should have been about to give birth? I became irritated at the mere mention of Christmas, and I just wanted to ignore everything associated with it. It seemed that in Alexa's absence, I had completely lost sight of everything she had taught me."

* * * * * * * *

LeNay rinsed out the deteriorating piece of steel wool in a bucket at her side, then she resumed her vigorous scrubbing of the stove. As long as she kept busy, it was easier to keep from thinking about anything that might provoke the pain and emptiness she was fighting so hard to avoid. Mrs. Higson had gone into town for her usual monthly shopping. Jesse had gone with his father to take care of some business. LeNay knew that he was well aware of her suffering, but she did her best to put up a brave front and not complain when he was around. Today, however, she felt worse than usual and was glad for his absence, fearing she didn't have the strength to hold her pain inside.

Mrs. Pace, the nanny who had been hired prior to Katherine's birth, had taken the child on a long walk. LeNay had always appreciated Mrs. Pace's help, in her non-interfering way. It had given LeNay the opportunity to be involved with Jesse's business. But she'd always done her best to see that Katherine remained the central focus of her life—until recently. Since she'd lost the baby, LeNay had found it more difficult to be patient with Katherine. But with the approach of Christmas nagging at her, the antics of a three-year-old seemed almost more than she could bear. She felt guilty, knowing that she was leaving her daughter in Mrs. Pace's care far too much, but she felt it was better than exposing Katherine to her mother's foul moods.

"Are you trying to clean it or kill it?" Jesse's voice startled her and she gasped.

"Both, perhaps," she said and concentrated on her scrubbing until Jesse took the tattered piece of steel wool from her, holding it gingerly between two fingers as if it was contaminated. He grimaced and tossed it into the garbage, saying, "Whatever it was, it's dead. I'm certain you could use a new piece. I think we can afford it."

LeNay knew he was trying to make her laugh, but she couldn't find the motivation. She picked up a rag and began wiping away the grime she'd loosened with the steel wool. "What are you doing here? I thought you'd be gone for hours yet."

"It went much more smoothly than we expected," Jesse said as he leaned against the counter and folded his arms over his chest. She sensed his concern but tried to ignore him. She was tired of trying to convince him that she was doing fine, when there was nothing either of them could do about it.

"Where's Katherine?" he asked.

"Mrs. Pace took her for a walk."

She heard Jesse sigh and could feel it coming. He was never critical of her, but his words stung with truth. "I think Katherine needs to spend more time with her mother."

"She is far better off elsewhere for the time being," LeNay said, still concentrating fully on improving the appearance of the stove. "If that child says the word 'Christmas' one more time, I'm going to scream."

"I thought you loved Christmas."

"I do. I did. I just . . ." LeNay pressed the back of a hand over her eyes as the unwanted emotion forced its way through. But Jesse's arms came around her, holding her as if he could somehow protect her from the pain.

"What?" he murmured. "Tell me." When she only cried he said, "Is it still the baby? Is it Grandma? What, LeNay? Tell me."

"It's everything," she cried. "Maybe if it was one or the other, I could make it. But how can I when . . ." She cried harder and he held her tighter. She expected him to try consoling her with words she'd heard a hundred times—words that seemed to make no difference. But instead he took her face into his hands, kissing her as if he could somehow draw her pain into himself where he could buffer it for her. LeNay responded eagerly, quickly losing herself in his affection. Her emotion dissipated into a familiar passion that somehow helped put everything into perspective. She gasped as he lifted her into his arms and moved into the hallway toward the stairs.

"What are you doing?" she demanded.

"I'm taking you upstairs," he said firmly. "What you need is some passionate lovemaking."

LeNay wiggled out of his arms at the foot of the stairs, noting his disconcerted expression. "I won't argue with that," she said a bit indignantly. "But I'll walk up the stairs on my own, thank you very much. The last thing I need is to have you keel over dead from a heart attack. And when it *does* happen, I'll not have it be from your carrying *me* around."

Jesse gave her a mild glare of disgust and she started up the stairs, holding his hand in hers. He followed her into the bedroom and locked the door.

"Do you think anyone will miss us?" he asked, sitting on the edge of the bed to pull off his boots.

"No," she said and eased into his arms.

Long after the passion had subsided into a perfect contentment, LeNay lay in her husband's embrace, gratefully distracted from the heartache that plagued her. Jesse maneuvered his hands through her hair and occasionally pressed a lingering kiss to her brow. "Are you feeling better?" he asked in a whisper.

"For the moment," she said, easing closer to him. "You always make everything better. Maybe that's part of the problem."

Jesse leaned up on one elbow to look at her, his brow furrowed. "Why is that a problem?"

LeNay touched his face and tears crept into her eyes. "What will I do when you're not here anymore? I have every reason to believe that I will outlive you by many years."

"We just have to live each day to its fullest and make the most of it," he murmured.

"I know that, Jesse. I do. But if it hurts this much to lose our grandmother, and a baby I never held, how can I possibly survive losing you?"

Jesse sighed and lay back on the pillow. "You know, LeNay," he said, "there is nothing I can say or do to change my heart problem. I can't promise you anything beyond the present, but then, can anyone? Any man could get run down on the street any day of the week and be killed. But I will not live out what life I have with this cloud of dread hanging over us. We've had some losses that have hurt us deeply. So be it. Life goes on. And we need to make the most of it."

LeNay moved away from him to get dressed, fearing she'd start sobbing uncontrollably otherwise. "If only it could be so easy," she said tersely. "You, who behaved completely irrationally when we lost Richard, have no right to tell me I'm not handling this well."

"I said no such thing," Jesse said, pulling on his breeches. "And my behavior when we lost Richard was wrong, LeNay."

"Your implications are very clear, Jesse. You think I don't know I'm having trouble with this?"

"Your grief is understandable, LeNay. But months have passed, and nothing seems to change. You're not going to find peace by carrying around this dark cloud. It's just not like you. If Alexa was here, she'd tell you that you need to have the faith to go on living and—"

"Well, Alexa *isn't* here. And that's the problem, isn't it."

"LeNay," Jesse softened his voice and took her shoulders into his hands, "I understand your pain, I do. But it's—"

"I'm not sure you do, Jesse," she interrupted, wishing it hadn't sounded so bitter.

"Okay, so maybe I don't completely understand. But I lost Alexa. And I lost a baby, too. But we have each other. And we have so much that's good; so much to be grateful for. You have a daughter who needs you. *I* need you. You have the ability to do so much good in this world. But no one can make that happen except you."

"And how am I supposed to do that? Do you think I can just snap my fingers and magically change the way I feel?"

"No, change comes slowly. But it doesn't happen unless you work at it."

"Okay. I'm listening," she said in a tone that clearly challenged him to give her a solution.

Jesse sighed and stuffed his hands into his pockets. She saw the muscles in his face twitch and knew that his patience was wearing thin. He gave a tense chuckle and said, "If I had known what kind of a stubborn woman I'd fallen in love with . . ."

"What?" she demanded.

He looked into her eyes. "Nothing. I would have married you anyway." He reached out a hand to touch her face. "I love you, LeNay. And I think if Alexa was here, she would tell you, just as she told me many times, that the only way to truly get beyond the things that get us down is to reach outside ourselves and give to others. What you do is up to you. But remember, you have a great impact on many people, most especially Katherine. And I think you're strong enough to get beyond this, for her sake if not for your own."

LeNay wanted to shout at him and tell him he had no idea what he was talking about. But truth rang through in his words—truth she didn't have the courage to look at. She wanted to just curl up in bed and stay there until next year. She wanted the world to just go away until she could wake up and not feel the emptiness. Knowing that was impossible, she turned away and left the room, wondering what Jesse Hamilton had ever seen in her to begin with.

For the next few days, LeNay managed to avoid being with anyone but herself for the most part. She was well aware of Jesse's frustration, but she didn't know what to do about it. She told him more than once that she loved him and appreciated his patience, but that didn't make the problem go away. She maneuvered herself out of the preparations for Christmas, and tried to ignore the decor being put up around the house. She tried to spend more time with Katherine, but the child talked incessantly of Father Christmas and all the fun she was anticipating for the holiday. It took great willpower for LeNay to keep from showing her resentment. Celebrating just didn't seem right under the circumstances. She knew the problem was within herself, but she didn't know how to fix it. So she did her best to ignore it.

On an especially hot afternoon, Jesse found LeNay scrubbing a bathtub, and he stood in the room for a full minute before he finally spoke. "Christmas is little more than a week away," he said.

"I know."

"You've done nothing to prepare or—"

"I know," she said more tersely.

"Do you think the holiday will just go by without you?"

"Yes. If I ignore it, it certainly will."

"And where does that leave me?" he asked, his voice cracking.

LeNay leaned back on her heels but didn't look at him. "The baby would have been due tomorrow," she said, as if that explained everything.

"I know," he said, and she heard him sniffle. She turned to see him wipe a hand over his face. He didn't cry easily, and for some reason, seeing him do it now made her feel a little less alone in her sorrow.

LeNay rinsed the cleanser off her hands and dried them before she put her arms around Jesse and just held him. She was trying to come up with a way to ask what was troubling him when he said quietly, "Lorinda Murphy came home from the hospital a while ago."

LeNay sighed and squeezed her eyes shut. Lorinda's hospital stay had been due to the birth of her new little son. LeNay was only vaguely acquainted with the stable-master's wife, but she couldn't help recalling the many times through the winter when they had compared pregnancy symptoms, since their babies were due about the same time. And now, the reality of Lorinda having a healthy baby boy seemed like lemon juice to sting LeNay's wounds. But she swallowed hard and asked, "How is she?"

"Not well, apparently." Jesse sat up straighter and wiped at his face. "Because he was born caesarean, she's apparently not feeling well at all. I mean, everything's fine, but . . . Murphy tells me it will take her some time to heal. He's concerned because he has that meeting in town tomorrow, and there isn't anyone else who can take his place. He doesn't want to leave her alone, but Mother and Lacey are pushing to get Christmas together for the boys, and it seems everyone is so busy, and . . ."

LeNay didn't realize she was glaring at her husband until he stopped talking abruptly. "What?" he demanded.

"If you're trying to ask me to go and help her, the answer is no."

Jesse's expression didn't alter even slightly. His tone was even as he stated, "I wouldn't ask you to do that. I know how hard it would be for you. I'm certain she'll manage. Mrs. Higson offered to check on her and . . ."

He stopped again, and LeNay knew that he was fighting emotion. She pressed her arms tightly around him, whispering gently, "What is it, Jesse?"

"I saw the baby," he said, then he chuckled tensely, as if to avoid sobbing. "He's sure a cute little thing. Lorinda says he looks like Murphy. I told her with any luck he'll grow out of that."

LeNay laughed softly at his joke, and the tension was eased somewhat. From the look in his eyes, she nearly expected him to start crying again, but he stood up abruptly, saying, "I really need to get back to work. I'll see you at supper."

LeNay watched him leave the room, then she sat down on the floor and cried.

Nothing more was said about the Murphys' new baby; not even at the supper table. The very fact that it didn't come up made LeNay certain the family was trying to spare her feelings—and perhaps Jesse's as well.

LeNay had trouble sleeping that night as thoughts of Lorinda and her new baby wouldn't relent. She finally drifted to sleep only to have crazy dreams, and she awoke with only one thought on her mind. If she didn't make some effort to help Lorinda Murphy, she could never live with herself. She knew well enough what it was like to have a new baby and not feel good enough to take care of it. But she'd had more help when Katherine was born than she'd known what to do with. Lorinda, however, was living out here in the middle of nowhere, far from family, where all but a few of the hired help were men. And those who were women were terribly busy with their occupations and preparations for the holiday.

Long after Jesse got up and left to get some work done before breakfast, LeNay lay there stewing over the situation. Then she slid to her knees next to the bed, almost against her will. As she put her mind to prayer, asking for the courage to face this necessary task, she couldn't recall the last time she'd prayed. Perhaps that in itself was part of the problem. As long as she was on her knees now, she asked God to help her get past these feelings that were causing problems for herself and those she loved. Then she came to her feet and took a deep breath, resigning herself to a situation that felt tantamount to jumping off a cliff.

LeNay walked slowly across the yard toward the old house, as they called it. The little home had been built by Jess Davies' father when he'd originally come here and claimed this land. After the big house had been built, this house had been used off and on for the overseer and his family, or whoever might need it. The home was currently occupied by Murphy, the stablemaster, who went only by his surname, like his father before him. And of course, his wife and their first child. LeNay knew they'd believed for many years that they'd never be able to have children, and they considered this baby a miracle. But it was difficult for her to acknowledge such a blessing when her own heart was aching.

LeNay took a deep breath as she approached the front door, wanting only to have this over with so she could at least say she'd made some effort and be free of the guilt plaguing her over the matter. She willed her hand to stop trembling as she lifted it to knock.

"Come in," she heard Lorinda call, and she stepped tentatively inside, closing the door behind her. "I'm in here," she added, and LeNay followed the voice toward the bedroom. "Forgive me for not getting up. I . . . Oh," she changed her tone of voice when LeNay appeared in the doorway. "Mrs. Hamilton." Lorinda looked tired and strained. Her eyes widened in such obvious surprise that LeNay couldn't help feeling guilty for her hesitance in coming. "I'm sorry," she said. "I just . . . didn't expect it to be you."

Following a tense moment of silence, LeNay forced a smile and said, "I wondered if I could . . . help you out some . . . while your husband's away."

Lorinda seemed speechless, perhaps even afraid. Was she thinking that LeNay should have had a baby too? Was she feeling awkward and wondering what to say, for the same reasons that LeNay was?

"That's very thoughtful of you," Lorinda said. "But I'm certain I can manage if . . ." She hesitated, and LeNay wanted to run away with some excuse, any excuse to leave. And Lorinda was giving her that option, as if she sensed her reluctance.

The baby began to fuss, startling LeNay to the realization that he was lying in a bassinet not far from the bed. Lorinda struggled to sit up, grimacing in spite of her obvious effort to conceal the pain.

"Here," LeNay said, hurrying across the room, "let me get him. You'll hurt yourself."

"Thank you," Lorinda said, and before LeNay gave it another thought, she realized she was holding the baby, looking down into his little round face.

"Oh, he's beautiful," LeNay muttered quietly, feeling something warm penetrate through her from holding the infant close.

"Yes, he is," Lorinda said.

LeNay lost herself in admiring the baby until his fussing became adamant. She set him carefully in Lorinda's arms so that he could be nursed, but it only took a minute for LeNay to realize that the new mother was having difficulty getting the baby to cooperate. As Lorinda's frustration became evident, LeNay sat on the edge of the bed and gave her some simple suggestions. The baby responded well and was soon nursing contentedly, while LeNay talked easily of her struggle to get Katherine to nurse through the first week or so of her life.

When nothing was said between them for a few minutes, LeNay put herself to straightening the room. She commented casually, "This is a nice home. It has a . . . quaint feel to it."

"Yes, it does," Lorinda said with enthusiasm. "I love it here. Did you know Alexa Davies lived here at one time?"

LeNay was genuinely surprised. "No, I didn't."

"Her first husband was Jess Davies' overseer, and they lived in this house until his death."

LeNay moved carefully to a chair, feeling suddenly overcome with a closeness to Alexa she'd not felt since her death. Absorbing a piece of information she'd never heard before, LeNay took in her surroundings again, trying to imagine Alexa living here. She was suddenly grateful to be here, if only to have experienced this feeling, even though it made missing Alexa closer to her heart.

When the baby was content but didn't seem prone to sleeping, LeNay offered to take care of him so Lorinda could get some rest. The new mother looked into LeNay's eyes, saying with intensity, "You don't have to do this. I know it must be hard for you, and—"

"I want to do this," LeNay said, surprised to realize she meant it. Holding the baby close, she stepped out of the bedroom and closed the door, realizing she'd just stepped outside herself for the first time since she'd lost her own baby.

Twelve
REUNION

It didn't take much effort for LeNay to find everything she needed to give the baby a bath, and she was surprised at how easily she managed when it had been so many years since Katherine had been an infant. Once he was bathed and dressed, she sat to rock him and he drifted easily to sleep. Holding him in her arms, LeNay finally lost the will to hold her emotion back. She cried for the ache inside of her at the loss of her own baby. She cried for missing Alexa, and all the wisdom and strength she had given. She cried for the fear she had of losing Jesse to premature death. The baby slept on, and LeNay just held him. Her thoughts turned to the death of her mother and the subsequent neglect and abuse by her father and his new wife. She realized that she'd not once spoken to her father since she'd left home five years ago. She wondered about her brothers and cried for them, too.

As one hour drifted into another and the tears flowed on, LeNay felt something change inside of her. Of all the tears she'd cried since Alexa's death, and the loss of her baby months later, none had been so cleansing. She felt a layer of peace and hope soothing the unbearable ache that had plagued her relentlessly. It was as if this child had somehow brought a little of heaven with him. And just holding him gave LeNay a perspective she'd been unable to see before now. Watching his little cherub face as he slept on, LeNay thought of the baby Jesus, who was the reason for the forthcoming celebrations. The peace that had begun to settle over her crept into every nerve, then crowded right into her heart. Suddenly it was easy to recall Alexa's gifts of hope and her admonitions of faith. LeNay now felt eager to celebrate the birth of the Christ child, with the hope in her heart that even if she wasn't destined to have a big family, she would one day be blessed with a son. And from somewhere deep inside, she found the faith to know that she could go on in spite of whatever this world dealt her. Life was rich and full, and she would enjoy every moment of it while it lasted. If Jesse's time here with her was brief, she would raise his children with the love and bounty he had brought into her life, and a prayer in her heart that they might one day be reunited in another time and place.

By the time the baby woke up, LeNay was feeling drained, yet somehow replenished. She took him to Lorinda when his fussing wouldn't be appeased. The new mother nursed him, more easily this time, then LeNay brought some lunch into Lorinda and they ate together in the bedroom. LeNay helped Lorinda get cleaned up and put on a fresh nightgown, then the baby wanted to nurse some more and LeNay made herself busy in the kitchen. She washed up all of the dirty dishes, then she worked her way through the house, straightening and doing a little cleaning. She peeked in on Lorinda a few times to find her resting with the baby sleeping beside her. In observing them, she had to take a moment to shed a few tears, but they were more of happiness for this little family than because of any bitterness for her own loss. As she returned to her cleaning, she was amazed to realize how a simple act of overcoming her fear enough to give of herself—even a little—had truly blessed her with the new perspective she was feeling.

Hearing a knock at the front door, LeNay hurried to answer it, hoping Lorinda wouldn't be disturbed. She was surprised to see her husband. "What are you doing here?" she asked as she stepped out onto the porch.

"I was going to ask you the same. We couldn't find you. I was getting worried."

"I told your mother where I would be."

"Mother just got back from town," he said with a furrowed brow and eyes that seemed concerned.

"I'm sorry," she said. "I didn't mean for you to worry. I just . . . thought I could make myself more useful here."

Jesse took her chin into his fingers and lifted her face to his view, as if he could read her eyes and spare himself from asking a difficult question. He finally said, "Are you okay?"

Tears brimmed in LeNay's eyes as she answered firmly, "Yes, actually, I am." She pressed herself into Jesse's arms, silently thanking God for all she'd been blessed with. Then she told him she'd be home for supper, once she saw that Lorinda had what she needed.

LeNay returned to her self-appointed chores, feeling some satisfaction in the good order of the little house, again imagining Alexa living here as a young woman. She wondered over the circumstances of her first marriage, and made a mental note to ask Emma about it sometime. After Mrs. Higson brought some supper over for Lorinda, LeNay returned home and ate with the family. She didn't know whether or not anyone noticed the changes in her, but she felt them surging through her and figured that was all that mattered.

When she was preparing for bed, Jesse commented, "You seem better."

"I am, yes," she said. They sat together in bed, and she told him all she'd felt this day. He got tears in his eyes when she expressed her hope that they would have a son, but whether or not they did, she was determined to enjoy every minute of her life with Jesse and make the most of it.

The following morning right after breakfast, LeNay visited Lorinda and found that her husband had finished up his business and would be checking on her between his minimal chores in the stables. She then went to the nursery and found Katherine playing in Mrs. Pace's care.

"Mama," Katherine said, running into LeNay's arms. She held her daughter tightly, resisting the urge to scold herself inwardly for her neglect of Katherine these past several weeks. The past couldn't be changed, but the present was hers to do with as she wished. And the future was whatever she made of it.

"How would you like to go into town today, my little angel?" she asked, and the child's eyes widened. "I thought we could buy some Christmas gifts and have lunch out."

"Can we buy a gift for Daddy?"

"Yes, of course," LeNay said.

"And Mrs. Pace, too?"

"Yes," LeNay laughed, winking at the nanny. "What would we ever do without Mrs. Pace?"

Through the drive into town, Katherine snuggled up close to LeNay's side, chattering constantly about her innocent perceptions of the world, and her perfect joy in anticipating the holiday. LeNay felt warmed to the core, and once again thanked God for all that was good in her life.

"Will we have birthday cake?" Katherine asked after a rare minute of silence.

"Is it somebody's birthday?" she inquired.

"Yes, it's Jesus's birthday. Will we have cake?"

LeNay laughed softly. "Well, I don't know that we'll actually have birthday cake. But we'll have plum pudding, and all kinds of wonderful things to eat. More importantly, when we celebrate Jesus's birthday, we do it by giving gifts to others, because that's what he taught us—to give to others. And when we give to others, it always makes us feel better."

The child nodded with understanding and LeNay smiled to herself, realizing that was exactly what she'd done yesterday. And it truly had made a difference.

Jesse walked out of the house to greet them when they returned from town. He laughed as Katherine jumped into his arms, chattering excitedly about all they had done. He smiled and winked at LeNay, then gave her a hug before they carried the packages into the house.

Later that evening, LeNay expressed to her husband a thought that had been prominently on her mind for much of the day. In the years she'd been here, she'd hardly given her father and brothers a second thought. Life had been full, and there had seemed no reason to. She doubted her father would have changed, and she couldn't feel any real desire to even speak with him. But suddenly she found herself wondering about her brothers. Where were they? Were they well? She'd not seen either of them since they'd left to fight the war; one had gone to Europe, the other to the Philippines.

"Well, why don't you just ring him up?" Jesse suggested.

"Who?"

"Your father."

"Because I don't want to talk to him."

"Okay. But he should know where your brothers are, right? If you can endure talking to him, you might at least be able to find out where they are. I'd like to meet them."

"You would?" she asked, and he laughed softly.

"They're your brothers, LeNay."

"I know but . . . they're so much older than I am, and I just feel as if they're strangers but . . . as you said, they are my brothers."

The following morning, LeNay walked out to the old house to check on Lorinda and the baby. She was feeling better and getting around more easily. They had a nice visit, and LeNay gave her a bottle of scented hand lotion she'd bought in town.

"Oh, it's lovely," Lorinda said. "Thank you."

"I remembered that you liked gardenias . . . from the first Christmas I was here."

Lorinda's eyes sparkled as she obviously recalled them sitting together at the Christmas feast nearly five years ago. LeNay held the baby while Lorinda took a bath, then she returned to the house to help Emma and Lacey with some Christmas preparations. The spirit of the holiday was in the air, and even more importantly, LeNay felt it within herself.

LeNay thought about her brothers long and hard, and five days before Christmas she finally got up the nerve to call her father's house. She almost hoped her stepmother would answer. As much as LeNay didn't like her, she felt sure she could get more information out of her with less drama. But her father answered the phone in his usual gruff voice. He didn't seem at all pleased to hear from her, and his only comment was, "If you're calling to get a handout, you've wasted your time, girl."

"I don't need a handout, Father, I can assure you. I was simply wondering how everyone's doing."

"We're fine," he said tersely.

"And what about Gary and Grant? Do you hear from them, or—"

"Gary was killed in the Philippines," he said in a voice that seemed to imply that LeNay's ignorance somehow put her at fault.

She sat down unsteadily and put a hand to her heart as she was struck with a reality she'd never even considered. Richard's death came to mind, and related emotions hovered close to the surface. LeNay hardly knew her brothers, but it was still difficult to accept that Gary was her brother, and he was dead.

"I . . . don't know what to say," LeNay finally managed to utter. "And . . . where is Grant? Is he—"

"He's an insolent fool. If it weren't for me, he'd be wandering the streets begging, not unlike yourself."

LeNay swallowed hard, resisting the urge to shout at her father in defense of herself. But she knew it wouldn't do any good. She wondered what he would think to know that she had married into one of the wealthiest families in Australia. Then she realized she didn't want him to know. She didn't care if she never saw him again. But she was concerned about Grant. What little had been said made her wonder what kind of situation he was in. And if her father was calling him an insolent fool, chances seemed high that he might have something in common with LeNay. Their father had once said similar things about her quite regularly.

"Do you know where I can reach him?" LeNay asked, fearing he wouldn't share any information.

"Of course I do. He's right here. Maybe you could take him off my hands for a while and—"

"Can I talk to him?" she interrupted, not wanting to listen to any more of her father's ranting.

"Fine," he said, then away from the phone, "It's your sister."

A different male voice said, "Hello" so quickly that LeNay knew he must have been right there, and likely had heard everything.

"Grant?" she asked tentatively, thinking he sounded very much like their father.

"LeNay?" came the reply.

"Yes," she said, and he laughed.

"I can't believe it. Where are you?"

"I'm living in Queensland. I'm married and have a daughter. How about you?"

Grant's voice was tense as he said, "Uh . . . it's just me. Things haven't been so good, but . . . well . . ."

He hesitated and she said, "Is it difficult to talk? Is Father right there?"

"Yes," he said, sounding relieved that she'd guessed the problem.

LeNay recalled what her father had said and impulsively offered, "Would you like to come and stay with us . . . for the holidays at least?"

206

"Oh, I don't think . . . well, I mean, just because of what he said . . . you don't have to feel like . . . I mean, I don't want to be a burden on you and—"

LeNay heard her father in the background, saying, "Better her than me. The two of you deserve each other."

"Please come," LeNay said. "Whatever's going on doesn't matter."

In the ensuing silence, LeNay prayed inwardly that she wasn't making a mistake, that she wasn't setting herself up for trouble. What if Grant had emotional problems? What if he was like her father? She reminded herself to at least give him a chance, and hoped that Jesse wouldn't think she'd been too presumptuous to offer such an invitation without his consent.

LeNay felt suddenly good about her offer when Grant said in a voice that cracked, "I'd love to, LeNay, but I . . . don't know how I'd get there, or—"

"I'll call you back in an hour," she said and hurried outside to find Jesse.

She was pleased when his response was simply, "Where is he? I can go get him tomorrow."

LeNay called Grant back, grateful when he answered the phone. She told him if he could get to the airport that was less than an hour away from where he was, they'd take care of the rest.

"I can do that," he said, "but . . . what do you mean?"

"My husband will pick you up . . . in his plane."

"Really?" Grant laughed.

"Pack light."

"That's not a problem. I don't have much."

"Okay, we'll see you tomorrow." She told him exactly when to meet Jesse, and hung up the phone feeling a childlike excitement. At supper she told the family her brother was coming for the holidays, and she was amazed at their genuine excitement—although she realized she shouldn't have been. Perhaps in the years she'd been here, she'd actually come to take their kindness for granted. Maybe her brother was one of those strays that needed a little boost from Byrnehouse-Davies and Hamilton. She prayed that whatever happened, all would go well.

The following morning very early, LeNay and Katherine walked Jesse out to his plane to send him off, then they returned to the house and LeNay helped wrap the gifts that Father Christmas would deliver to the boys at the usual Christmas Eve celebration. She thought of her brother being there, and felt so warm inside that she couldn't hold back a little laugh.

"Is something funny?" Emma asked.

"No, I was just thinking of the fun we'll have Christmas Eve. I do hope my brother fits in well. I haven't seen him for years. In fact, I hardly know him."

"I'm sure everything will be fine," Emma said.

"It would seem," Lacey added, "that you've taken after your grandmother rather well."

"My grandmother?"

"Alexa," Lacey said. "She *is* your grandmother too, you know." The thought warmed LeNay even more. "And just like her," Lacey went on, "you have a big heart."

LeNay glanced down timidly, certain Lacey's praise was grossly exaggerated. She simply said, "I have many good examples of kindness. I am truly blessed."

"We all are, love," Emma said. "We just want to spread it around as much as possible. I'm truly glad your brother is coming."

"So am I," LeNay said.

When supper was over and Jesse hadn't returned yet, LeNay decided to go riding at Emma's suggestion, if only to ease her nerves. Wearing riding breeches and the boots Jesse had bought her the Christmas before they were married, she galloped a spirited stallion through the fields around the house, listening for the plane. She began to worry that something might have gone wrong when the sun started to set and they hadn't arrived. She wondered if perhaps Jesse had had trouble finding him. Or maybe Grant hadn't been able to get to the airport. Or far worse, what if they'd had trouble, or been in an accident?

She nearly returned to the house to see if Jesse might have called, then she heard the plane in the distance and her heart quickened. Each time he flew in when she was out in the field, she was reminded of the time he'd come home Christmas Eve, when she'd wondered if she'd ever see him again.

Seeing the plane as it appeared over the horizon, LeNay laughed aloud and galloped toward it. It swept down out of the sky and turned in a wide sweep, then Jesse flew almost alongside her, as if they were racing. It certainly wasn't the first time he'd done such a thing, but the thrill never lessened. The man seated in the plane with Jesse waved with enthusiasm, and she waved back. LeNay didn't get a good look at her brother, and it would have been difficult to recognize him with the goggles he wore. But the anticipation of seeing him enhanced the excitement she felt as the plane made a smooth landing and came to a stop in the field. LeNay dismounted and held the reins as Jesse stepped down from the plane, then he turned to help her brother step down from the wing.

Something stabbed at LeNay's heart as she realized Grant was having difficulty getting down, then Jesse put a cane into his hand before they moved slowly toward her. Jesse held a piece of luggage in one hand, and kept hold of Grant's arm with the other.

As they approached very slowly, the warmth that had been hovering inside LeNay since she'd held Lorinda Murphy's baby suddenly swelled with such enormity that she couldn't hold back a rush of tears. The familiarity of her brother quickly became evident, but he'd aged significantly since she'd seen him. She felt certain that the war and whatever had happened since had been hard on him. When they were finally standing face to face, LeNay simply said, "Hello, Grant."

"Hello, LeNay," he said, with that same crack in his voice she'd heard over the phone. She sensed some hesitancy in him, but she embraced him firmly anyway. She was surprised when he held to her tightly, then she realized he was crying. Returning his embrace eagerly, LeNay looked over his shoulder to see Jesse's warm smile.

"Come along," LeNay said, taking her brother's arm as Jesse had done. She ignored his emotion as they moved on toward the house. "We have a room ready for you, and you need to meet the rest of the family."

"This place is incredible," he said, looking around with an expression of awe.

"Yes, it is," LeNay said and slipped her other hand into Jesse's. "You'll soon find that it's something close to heaven."

"That must explain it, then," Grant said.

"Explain what?"

"Well . . . do you remember what Mother used to tell us? If you're ever in trouble, all you have to do is pray, and God will send an angel to guide you."

"I remember," she said, feeling a sudden warmth rush over her shoulders as she stopped walking to face her brother. How could she forget thinking that very thing when Alexa had found her on the streets?

"Well, I was beginning to wonder if God existed at all. But now I know that he does. Just when I didn't think I could go on another day, an angel called on the phone." He laughed softly and glanced toward Jesse. "And now I've flown into heaven itself, it would seem."

Jesse laughed. "You might not feel that way once we put you to work."

Grant laughed too, and LeNay said, "Work? But he just got here, and—"

"We'll talk about it later," Jesse said. "Let's get some supper, Grant. Shall we?"

After Grant had been shown to his room and left to freshen up, Jesse told LeNay, "Your brother's a wonderful man. I shouldn't wonder." He smiled and gave her a quick kiss. "Since he has nowhere to go at the moment, I offered him a job once the holidays are over. I hope that's okay."

"Of course. It's wonderful, but what—"

"Let's go eat, I'm starving. We'll talk later."

LeNay's curiosity about her brother's circumstances wasn't satisfied until after Grant and Jesse were given something to eat, then they went out to the veranda where Michael, Emma, Tyson, and Lacey were sitting. They were gracious and warm toward Grant as introductions were made, then they sat and visited for a long while before Grant's circumstances came up. LeNay fought to keep her emotion in check as her brother told the story of how he'd married a woman during leave while he was serving in the army.

"Even though it happened quickly," Grant said, "I believed our love was strong and true. But when I returned with my leg barely intact, she just didn't seem the same. Of course, we were practically strangers. But after the third surgery, she basically told me this wasn't the life she'd expected. I haven't been able to work, and I had no choice but to stay with Father for the time being. But honestly, if I'd had to stay there much longer, I'd have gone insane. I've felt so lost and alone that . . ." His voice broke, and LeNay realized that with the intensity of emotion he'd displayed both on the phone and since his arrival, his frame of mind was likely more desperate than he'd admit to. "Well," he added, taking LeNay's hand, "let's just say your call was an answer to prayers, even though I hardly dared believe they would be heard at all." He kissed her hand and looked into her eyes. Then he turned to Jesse, speaking as if they'd been friends forever. "My sister's an angel, you know. Just like her mother."

"Yes, I know," Jesse said with a warm smile.

Through the following days, as the traditional Christmas celebrations unfolded, LeNay found an added joy in observing Grant's obvious enchantment with all that was taking place. She couldn't help recalling her first Christmas here, and how incredible all of this had seemed to her. She recalled the hope Alexa had given her then, and realized now that even in Alexa's absence, all she had taught through her example and wisdom was still strong in LeNay's heart.

Grant took to calling LeNay his angel, and each time he said it she was reminded of the way she'd thought of Alexa as an angel when she'd found LeNay on the street and taken her home. She told the story to her brother during a quiet moment, and she found a growing closeness to him that made the loss of her baby seem less painful. As she told Grant about Alexa and all this great woman had taught her, she recognized that one of Alexa's greatest qualities was her ability to give of herself. She'd been blessed with a good life and a great deal of abundance, and she had spent her life passing it around through simple acts of charity that had seemed as natural to Alexa as breathing. And now LeNay could see that with very little effort, she had been able to do the same for others. When all was said and done, she could see clearly why Alexa had been able to find so much joy in her life, even in Jess's absence. And why she had been able to have so much faith and hope. Her ability to give to others had kept everything else in its proper perspective. And with the ring of Christmas in the air, LeNay knew that the gifts Alexa had passed out so freely in her life truly encompassed the spirit of the holiday. LeNay was determined to live her life with Alexa as her mentor. Until her dying breath, she would do her best to live with faith, hope, and charity as her guiding lights. Just as Alexa had done.

* * * * * * * *

LeNay reached her feeble fingers toward Allison, who took them and squeezed gently, wiping at her tears with her other hand. "I still miss Alexa, you know," LeNay said in a voice that was strained and obviously weary. Allison sensed the end of their time together drawing near, and she dreaded having to be separated from these hours that would forever be among the most treasured of her life.

"She was an incredible woman," Allison said. "Much like you."

"I've truly tried to live the way she would have me live," LeNay said. "But I still believe that Alexa had a special something about her that was . . . well, in some ways I think she was truly an angel."

Allison watched her grandmother in awe. While she was humbly talking about Alexa with such adoration, Allison felt exactly the same way about LeNay. Something inside her wanted to emulate LeNay's goodness and wisdom, just as LeNay had done with Alexa's. "You are an angel, Grandma," Allison said, finding it impossible to hold back her tears. "Just like your brother said you were."

LeNay laughed softly and gave a humble smile, then she drifted almost instantly to sleep, as if she was completely exhausted. Allison turned off the recorder and watched her grandmother sleeping. She looked tenuous and frail, and it wasn't difficult to believe that her time left on this earth would be very brief. With silent tears coursing continually down her cheeks, Allison recalled the stories she'd heard through their intermittent hours together, marveling at the love and strength that had been passed from one generation to another.

It was easy for Allison to fit the remainder of the story together in her mind. Jesse and LeNay had been blessed with a son, Michael, who had married Allison's mother. Allison thought of all the love and generosity Michael had given them through the years. And now she understood its source.

While LeNay slept on, Allison sat where she was, not wanting to break the ethereal mood surrounding her. She pondered the stories all over again: Jesse and LeNay.

Michael and Emma. Tyson and Lacey. Richard. And, of course, Jess and Alexa. Allison finally left the room and wandered idly through the house, grateful beyond words for the day Alexa had come here in 1888 to ask Jess Davies for a job.

EPILOGUE

The Present

Allison found it ironic that LeNay was suddenly sleeping most of the time, when she'd been so perky with stories and memories. It was as if she'd completely exhausted herself, or perhaps she felt her time here was done. Perhaps both. She acknowledged family members as they arrived and greeted her, but beyond that she seemed content to sleep.

Allison felt her emotions hovering close to the surface as the usual Christmas celebrations unfolded. She marveled to observe these traditions that were so familiar to her, and to realize that they hadn't changed even slightly since LeNay had come here in 1942. It was especially difficult to keep from visibly crying as she walked alongside the horse-drawn wagon to the boys' home for the traditional Christmas Eve festivities, and the arrival of Father Christmas.

"Who is that, really?" Allison whispered in Michael's ear.

"It's Murphy, of course," he said with a little smirk, and Allison realized this was the baby born to Lorinda Murphy in LeNay's story.

On the evening of Christmas Day, when all the celebrating was finished and the house was cloaked in a quiet reverie, Allison sat by LeNay's bedside, holding her hand while she slept. She knew she needed to go to sleep herself. They would be leaving early in order for her to make her flight home. This would be her last opportunity to be with her grandmother, but the feeling surrounding them was calm and serene. And her gratitude was deep.

Allison was pleased when LeNay awoke, smiling peacefully when she realized Allison was there. "Is there a little box there on the table?" she asked.

"What, this?" Allison asked, picking up a little jewel box of burgundy velvet.

"Yes," LeNay said in a faint voice. "I had your mother get this out for me. I want you to have it. Open it."

Allison gasped as the box opened to reveal the tear-shaped diamond on a gold chain—the one Alexa had given her in 1943. "Oh, Grandma, I couldn't possibly. It's so—"

"Now, listen to me, Allison. You have been a very big bright spot in my life. And my life is nearly over. I want you to have this, and I hope you will remember something of what Alexa taught me."

"I will," Allison said, tearfully hugging her grandmother. "Thank you. I'll treasure it always, but . . ." She sniffled and wiped at her tears. "But not nearly so much as everything else you've given me."

LeNay smiled again, then drifted back to sleep. Allison sat there lost in thought until Michael's voice startled her, and she looked up to see him standing in the doorway. "She's told me five times how glad she is that you came."

"I'm glad I came, too," Allison said. She pressed a kiss to her grandmother's cheek and left the room with her father so they wouldn't disturb LeNay's rest with their conversation. He put his arm around her as they moved idly down the long hall.

"Your father was an incredible man," she said, thinking of Jesse Hamilton.

"Yes, he was," Michael said, then he embarked on a barrage of memories of his father. They ended up on the sofa in the library, talking for a long while. Then their conversation turned to Michael's grandparents.

"You remember them, then?" Allison asked.

"Oh, yes. Michael and Emma both outlived my father, actually. They were incredible people."

"Did you know Tyson and Lacey, too?"

"Oh, yes," he said.

"Tell me about them," she said eagerly. She felt she knew the story of Jess and Alexa well, but these people still seemed vague to her, and she knew they had some fascinating stories in their lives as well.

But Michael glanced at the clock and said, "It's going to have to wait. If we don't get to bed, we won't make it. You can sleep on the plane, but I've got to fly it, you know."

His comment brought on a whole new perspective for Allison. "Did you fly with your father?"

"I did," Michael said. "Now, to bed with you. We'll talk later."

Allison appreciated his promise, but even their long flight in the morning would hardly seem adequate to glean from him the information she desperately wanted to hear.

The following morning, Allison told LeNay good-bye, even though she was sleeping soundly. It was evident from the brief periods she was conscious that she wouldn't hang on much longer. Allison forced herself to not think too much about that. Her family members were all there to see her off, in spite of the early hour. As always, it was most difficult to say good-bye to her mother. Emily hugged Allison tightly, and tears came to her eyes as Allison got into the Cruiser with Michael and they drove toward the hangar.

Flying in the private plane with Michael took on new meaning for Allison in light of LeNay's stories. Michael shared his memories of family members while Allison hung on every word, feeling them come to life a little more in her mind. The flight had never seemed so short, and she found it more difficult than usual to tell him good-bye and get on the 747 that would take her to the States.

"Here," Michael said after they'd shared a long embrace.

"What is it?" Allison said, taking a little computer diskette from his hand.

Michael smiled slyly, saying, "I've transcribed all of the family journals, a little at a time, over the years. This is everything written by Michael and Emma, and Tyson and Lacey. It's just a little extra Christmas gift."

Allison laughed through a sudden rush of tears and hugged Michael again.

Through the long flight home, Allison couldn't help feeling overwhelmed and overjoyed. The opportunity to spend Christmas at home with her family had been wonderful, but the highlight for her had been the time she'd spent with LeNay. She thought of the tapes tucked into her bag, and the priceless information they held. She couldn't wait to read the diskette her father had given her, but she doubted she would get to it until Valentine's Day, thinking of all she had to do at home. At least it would give her something to look forward to. She felt as if there was an adventure just around the corner in being able to discover the details of Michael and Emma's lives, as well as Tyson and Lacey's.

Allison's thoughts went back to LeNay. She shed some tears, knowing she'd never see her grandmother again—at least not in this life. But she thought of the priceless gift LeNay had given her; of the faith, hope, and charity that she had passed down from Alexa, emphasizing their meaning by the tender stories she'd told of her past. Allison challenged herself to apply those things in her own life more fully. She touched the teardrop necklace around her throat, and thought of LeNay wearing it to the dance the night Jesse had confessed his love to her. She imagined Jesse Hamilton waiting for his sweet LeNay now, and felt peace in thinking of them being reunited, and the celebration they would likely share. Then she thought of Ammon waiting at the airport to pick her up, and the Christmas festivities that had been postponed until her return. She found the two situations somehow similar, and a deep warmth filtered through her, like the spirit of Christmas encompassing a child. Allison rubbed the chill from her arms and looked out the window of the plane. "I'm flying," she whispered. Then she laughed.

ABOUT THE AUTHOR

Anita Stansfield published her first LDS romance novel, *First Love and Forever,* in the fall of 1994, and the book was winner of the 1994-95 Best Fiction Award from the Independent LDS Booksellers. Since then, her best-selling novels have captivated and moved thousands of readers with their deeply romantic stories and focus on important contemporary issues. *The Three Gifts of Christmas* is her thirteenth novel to be published by Covenant.

Anita has been writing since she was in high school, and her work has appeared in *Cosmopolitan* and other publications. She and her husband, Vince, and their five children and two cats live in Alpine, Utah.

PROLOGUE

South Queensland, Australia—1879

Jess Davies rode through the night with fury. His brief journey had done nothing but confirm a truth he hadn't wanted to hear. He could feel the stallion's exhaustion. But Jess almost believed the horse understood this need he had to ride fast and hard, as if the speed could somehow drive away his anguish.

Jess thought of his mother. He couldn't talk to her about this. Her fragile mind would never endure it. But the miles passed more easily as he imagined her at the piano. He wanted to just sit and listen to her play, or to breathe the smell of oils while she dabbed paint onto the canvas. He ached to sit across the dinner table from her, and feel the normalcy of life that had always been there, as if it could somehow dispel the horror of what he'd learned earlier today. He knew now what had destroyed her mind, and the thought made bile rise into his throat. He concentrated instead on the moonlit landscape as it became familiar. And he hurried on. He was almost home.

An acrid smell teased the night air. Jess reined the horse in sharply and checked the wind's direction. *Smoke.*

He inhaled and coughed while the stallion danced beneath him, eager to run. With little urging the animal broke into a gallop, as if it sensed the panic that made Jess's heart pound into his throat, where it threatened to choke him.

Jess halted at the hilltop, and his little remaining hope crumbled to ashes. Surely it was his imagination! He was tired and distraught. A forefinger and thumb rubbed eyes that ached from sleeplessness and stung from the thickening haze. He blinked away the mist in his eyes and focused on a rosy luster gleaming against the black horizon, illuminating the night like a torch rising from hell.

"No!" Jess cried and pressed the stallion mercilessly. His home was that torch.

Jess expected to find the station in a flurry, all hands attempting to douse the fire. But a deathly stillness greeted him, broken only by the hiss and crackle of the consuming flames. A reddish glow reflected off the somber faces of his hired hands. Hopeless eyes turned toward Jess as he dismounted, posing silent questions that no one dared answer.

"We tried, Jess," Murphy muttered hoarsely, his blackened face streaked with perspiration.

Jess turned his gaze to the rising inferno and heard lumber crash inside the house. Sparks flew into the smoke-darkened sky and he stepped back warily, fearing the entire structure would collapse any minute. Sweat beaded over his face from the intensity of the heat, and he mopped it with the back of his sleeve.

"Where's my mother?" Jess asked, his eyes fixed on the looming fire. When no one responded, he turned loose the fury of his fears. "Where is she?!" he bellowed, taking Murphy by the collar to shake the words out of him.

"Richard tried to get her out," he cried. "We all did our best, but . . . it happened so fast and . . ."

"Where is she?" Jess shook him again.

"She didn't make it, Jess," Murphy croaked.

Jess stared in disbelief until the reality stormed through him and he fell to his knees. "No!" he groaned from deep in his chest, covering his face with his hands. "Please, no!" he howled toward the sky. But it was lost in the din as the roof crashed into the house, and the surrounding flames lapped higher in triumph.

Through the following day, Jess's agony subsided into a numb grief. Everything that mattered to him had gone up in smoke. By evening light he sifted through the barely cool pile of burned rubble, the ashes of his father's dream house. Despite the relief that his father wasn't here to see this, a part of him ached for Benjamin Davies' strength and courage.

Jess couldn't believe the thorough destruction. He found nothing recognizable that he might hold or touch to muster up a good memory. Wanting to be free of the nightmarish surroundings, he closed his eyes. But all he could see were horrifying images of freshly turned graves, and the unsightly burns that now defiled Richard, his closest friend.

"Why?" he groaned, and the answer pounded through his head with perfect clarity. *Chad Byrnehouse.*

Jess dropped a charred plank and strode with vengeance toward the stables. He wiped his sooty hands on his breeches and bridled a spirited gelding. With a racing saddle beneath him, Jess thundered over the miles of Australian terrain to where his land met that of Byrnehouse. The speed drove Chad's heated words through his mind: *I'll see you fail. You will never win another race. Your mother will regret ever bearing you.*

225

It had been less than two weeks since Chad had uttered his ruthless threats. Already Jess's mother lay dead, and his world smoldered in a mass of charcoal. Coincidence? Gut instinct told him *no*.

Sweat rose over Jess's lip as he waited in the polished entry hall. The evidence of wealth sickened him as he pictured what remained of his own home. Anger tightened his throat when Chad sauntered down the stairs, glaring at Jess with disdain.

"What do *you* want?" Chad sneered.

"You filthy, murderous swine!" Jess muttered as his fist connected with Chad's face.

Blood spewed from Chad's nose, but he recovered quickly and lunged in retaliation. Jess dodged to the right and grabbed Chad by the collar, slamming him against the door.

"Why?" Jess asked through clenched teeth. Chad didn't answer, and Jess slammed him again. "You tell me what I ever did to you to deserve such contempt."

"You were born," Chad growled, wiping at the blood on his face.

Jess pulled back to strike again. Chad blocked it with a forearm and hit Jess across the jaw. Jess fell back briefly, but his motivation urged him on. In his head, he heard his mother screaming as flames engulfed her. Chad doubled over from the fist in his stomach, then reeled backward as Jess struck his lower jaw. Before Chad found his footing, Jess knocked him across the side of the head and threw him to the floor, holding him there with the weight of his body, his hands firmly around Chad's throat. Chad struggled and gasped for breath, but Jess only tightened his grip. "I'm going to kill you," he muttered. "I swear I'll kill you."

Jess ignored the hand on his shoulder and concentrated on the changing color of Chad's skin. He fought against the arms attempting to drag him off, until Tyson Byrnehouse shook him hard and shouted in his ear, "Jess!"

Jess loosened his grip but remained as he was.

"Get him off me!" Chad managed to utter. "He's as crazy as his mother!"

Jess tightened his hold and shook Chad. He *felt* crazy. All he could think of was seeing Chad suffer.

"Jess!" Tyson took Jess by the shoulders. "Stop this madness. Listen to me."

Jess ignored the intrusion. He wanted only one thing.

"Jess," Tyson repeated quietly, "I understand how you must be feeling, but if your father were alive, I don't believe he would be so brash."

Jess met the eyes hovering above him as confusion pressed into his brain. Chad's father wasn't a man Jess liked, but he respected him. "What would you know about that? You hated my father."

"And he hated me, I know," Tyson admitted, a tinge of regret in his voice. "But perhaps he's been gone long enough for me to admit that he was a good man." Tyson spoke quickly, as if he feared Chad might stop breathing. "I knew him, Jess. I know he taught you right, and . . ."

A clear image of Ben Davies appeared in Jess's mind, and he relinquished his grip as if his hands had been burned. Ben's example of strength and discipline was the only thing that gave Jess any peace at all.

"And he loved you," Tyson finished with a breathy sigh. Jess lumbered to his feet as Chad fought to catch his breath.

"So he did," Jess said with a bitter edge. These people didn't know the half of it. In that moment he wished his father hadn't been so adamant about turning the other cheek. But personal experience had made Ben Davies a man who abhorred violence, especially for the sake of vengeance. Despite Jess's fury, how could he blatantly ignore his father's dying admonition to find peace with his enemies? The only enemy Ben ever had was Tyson Byrnehouse. Jess felt as torn as if he were locked in some ancient torture device.

As Tyson helped Chad to his feet, Jess noticed the sooty handprints around Chad's throat. He glanced down at himself and was reminded of the blackened mess his life had become. He met the glare in Chad's eyes and felt the urge for vengeance returning. He was almost relieved when Chad lunged toward him, ready to have it out again. But Tyson stepped between them. "You watch yourself, Chad," he admonished, "or you'll have me to deal with."

Chad backed down reluctantly, but Jess kept a wary eye on him. Tyson turned sternly toward Jess, and he felt certain he'd get a lecture. As a youth, he had crossed this man more than once.

"We were sorry to hear," Tyson said with compassion.

"Yeah, sorry," Chad smirked. Jess clenched his fists.

"Might I guess what this is all about?" Tyson asked coolly. Jess said nothing. "Is it possible you believe Chad had something to do with that fire?"

Jess's jaw went tight and his heart beat painfully. How could he tell this man his son was guilty of arson and murder?

"If there is another reason you were trying to kill Chad, just say so." Tyson lifted a terse eyebrow.

"I've reason to believe Chad's responsible," Jess muttered, "if that's what you want to know."

Jess expected him to question this, but Tyson took it at face value and turned to Chad. "Well?"

"Well what?" Chad retorted as if he didn't have a clue what they were talking about.

"If you had something to do with that fire, you'd best speak up now or the trouble will just get deeper."

Chad looked astonished at the accusation, but Jess caught the brief, unmistakable fear that passed through his eyes. "Oh, come now," Chad chuckled as if it were ridiculous. "You can't honestly believe that I would . . . do something so . . . *barbaric.*"

"I would certainly hope not," Tyson said, "but I'm asking anyway."

"Well, I didn't," Chad defended angrily, then he turned prideful eyes on Jess. "And even if I did, you could never prove it."

Jess mustered every bit of self-control he possessed to keep from attacking Chad all over again. Instead he turned to Tyson, knowing full well he'd protect his son.

"I don't think there's anything more we can do," Tyson stated. "We'll just pass this off to the rage of youth, and—"

"Pass it off?" Jess protested. "I'm nineteen years old! I've been running my own station for a year and a half, since my father died. My mother and two servants have been killed and my house burned to the ground. This is not some adolescent fight out behind—"

"Jess." Tyson raised a hand to stop him. "It was an accident. Things like that just happen. It's tragic, but nothing is going to change it."

"That's true," Chad chimed in.

Tyson glared at him. "Get out of here," he ordered.

Chad's eyes filled with defiance, but he only stared hard at Jess and skulked away.

Alone with Tyson Byrnehouse, Jess felt less than adequate. Tyson's stature alone demanded respect, but Jess was surprised to note that he met him eye to eye. Had it been so many years since they'd spoken?

Tyson slowly lifted a finger. "Leave it alone, Jess," he whispered. It nearly sounded like a threat. Was it possible that Tyson also had something to do with this? Jess looked him in the eye and felt sure he didn't. But perhaps he knew why Chad was so bent on destruction.

Tyson was quiet for a moment. He seemed different in Chad's absence. His eyes softened, and he spoke to Jess with grave sincerity. "There is no good to be had in irrational vengeance, Jess. It will always come back to you, and there is no pain so great as living with the truth of your own mistakes." He put a hand on Jess's shoulder, and the wisdom in his words was as real as the despair in his eyes. "No matter how unjustly you've been treated, if you start fighting fire with fire, you'll get burned." Tyson lowered his chin and added firmly, "And in my opinion, you're too much of a man for that."

Tyson patted Jess on the shoulder as if they'd just had a friendly chat at the track. His penetrating gaze pierced Jess once more, then he turned and walked away, leaving Jess stunned. The look in Tyson Byrnehouse's eyes was something he'd never forget. There was nothing he could do now but go home—if what remained of it could be called such.

As Jess turned toward the door, his eyes caught movement. Looking up, he noticed a pair of tiny legs, clad in breeches and riding boots, dangling from the stairs. The face of a child with short-cropped hair peered timidly between the bannister posts. As soon as their eyes made contact, the little girl scampered away, and Jess wondered how much she had witnessed.

The ride home dragged as Jess kept the horse at a gentle walk. While he contemplated the severity of Tyson Byrnehouse's words, thoughts of his parents clouded his mind. He longed for his mother's comfort and his father's sound wisdom. But reality had to be faced: Jess was alone, and he could only try to do what they might have wanted him to.

Jess had no idea of the time as he left the gelding in the stable and went to the bunkhouse. The boys were gathered around the table where they usually played dice or cards. But there were no games, no evidence of anything beyond mourning.

"Blimey!" Murphy noticed Jess first as he closed the door behind him. "What happened to you?"

Jess touched his lip and felt the dried blood. "Oh," he grumbled, "I had a little talk with Byrnehouse."

"Who won?" Jimmy almost smiled.

"I think I won the fight," Jess said gravely, "but I'm afraid I lost the war."

"Do you think he did it?" Murphy asked.

"I *know* he did it, but there's not one thing I can do about it."

Silence confirmed this as common knowledge. The Byrnehouses were wealthy and powerful, one being a result of the other.

"How is he?" Jess glanced toward the other room where Richard lay.

"'Bout the same," Murphy reported. "That stuff the doc gave him keeps him out most o' the time."

231

"Just as well," Jess mumbled and stepped quietly to Richard's bedside. Though Richard slept, it was evident that pain still plagued him by the way he moaned and writhed. Jess sat carefully on the edge of the bed and put a comforting hand on his shoulder. Gingerly he lifted the edge of the bandage that covered the left side of Richard's face. What he'd hoped would look better was worse. Jess grimaced at the thought of what Richard's life would be like as a result of this tragedy. It was one more reason to hate Chad Byrnehouse, and to wonder if he could live with letting it go.

"I don't know if you can hear me, my friend," Jess said in the most positive tone he could manage, "but we're going to start over. We're going to rebuild. And somehow we're going to make it work."

Richard made no response, and Jess leaned his face into his hands. He didn't feel convinced. The same gut instinct that told him Chad Byrnehouse was responsible nagged him to believe this was not the last of it.